Matthew Kneale

When We Were Romans

Matthew Kneale was born in London in 1960, the son of two writers. He is the author of numerous prizewinning novels, including the bestselling *English Passengers*, which won the Whitbread Award and was shortlisted for the Booker Prize. He lives with his wife and two children in Rome.

When We Were Romans

When We Were Romans

- a novel -

MATTHEW KNEALE

Anchor Books
A Division of Random House, Inc.
New York

FIRST ANCHOR BOOKS EDITION, AUGUST 2009

Copyright © 2007 by Matthew Kneale

All rights reserved. Published in the United States by Anchor Books, a division
of Random House, Inc., New York. Originally published in Great Britain by
Picador, London, in 2007, and subsequently published by arrangement with
Picador in hardcover in the United States by Nan A. Talese, a division of
Random House, Inc., New York, in 2008.

Anchor Books and colophon are registered trademarks of Random House, Inc.

The Library of Congress has cataloged the Nan A. Talese edition as follows:
Kneale, Matthew.
When we were Romans : a novel / Matthew Kneale.—1st ed. in
the U.S. of America.
p. cm.
1. Problem families—Fiction. 2. English—Italy—Fiction.
3. Rome (Italy)—Fiction. I. Title.
PR6061.N37W47 2008
823'.914—dc22 2007045523

Anchor ISBN: 978-0-307-38786-8

Book design by Gretchen Achilles

www.anchorbooks.com

Printed in the United States of America
10 9 8 7 6 5 4 3 2 1

For my father, who taught me so much about how to build a story.

When
We Were
Romans

CHAPTER ONE

One day scientists found something strange out in space. This thing was pulling millions of galaxies towards it, one of them is the Milky Way which is ours, but the scientists couldn't see the thing because it was hidden behind lots of dust. They thought "this thing must be huge to pull all these galaxies towards it, and we are getting pulled towards it really fast, it is at millions of miles per hour, but it could be anything, nobody knows, it is a mystery." They thought "this is strange, this is scary" and then they said "I know, let's call the thing the Great Attractor."

The great Attractor is pulling us right now. I think it is probably a huge black hole, because black holes eat everything, they even eat light so you can't ever see them, they look just like a piece of really dark night. One day I bet there will be a big disaster, we will go nearer and nearer and then suddenly we will get pulled right in. It will be like a big hand gets us so we will vanish, because nothing can get out of a black hole you see, we will be stuck there for ever. It is strange to think that every day, every minute we are all being pulled towards the Great Attractor but hardly anybody knows. People go about their ordinary every day lives, they have toast for breakfast and go to school, they watch their favorite programs on the telly and they never even guess.

We were coming back from the supermarket, we went to a further away one where we never went before so it would be all right, and it was an adventure mum said, we must be really quick, we must be like birds diving down and getting some food and flying away with it in their mouths. It was fun, actually, we got our cart and we almost ran, we just grabbed all the tins and packets and milk and tinfoil etc etc. Then Jemima saw some sweets in a little purple tin and she said "oh I want them, I need them, please mum." Mum said "don't be silly now, Lamikin" which is what she calls Jemima sometimes "anyway those aren't real sweets their cough sweets, their bad for you." But Jemima didn't listen, she never does, and she started crying like a big crybaby, she said "but I need them, I need that purple tin."

She was still saying it when we were coming back in the car and suddenly we were almost home. We went past Mrs Potters house and the droopy trees which look funny like hair and I thought "uhoh" I thought "now there will be trouble" but I didn't say anything of course, because we couldn't ever say anything in front of Jemima, because she was too young to understand. But then there was a surprise, because it was fine after all. Jemima was terrible just like I expected, when mum stopped the car she said "I'm staying here, I want to go back to the supermarket" but mum was ready, she said "if you come with me then I'll give you a nice treat" and it worked. Jemima went quiet and said "all right." Then we were so fast. Mum got Jemima out of her car seat and we all got all the plastic bags out of the trunk, I carried lots, even though they were really heavy, we went to the door, we were almost running, and Mum had her key all ready. That was when I looked round, I didn't really want to but I couldn't help it, I just had to. I looked at the fence and the bushes. But it was all all right, there wasn't anybody at all.

Then we were inside, mum shut the door, she locked it, and I thought "hurrah hurrah" I thought "look at all this food, this will last ages." We put it away in the fridge and the cupboards, and after that I went up to see Hermann. I cleaned his bowls and gave him some new nuts and water. Jemima followed like always so I let her watch, I said "no you can't hold him." Then it was time for robot wars, which is one of my favorite programs, there was a robot called the obliterator and another called the stamper which had a big sort of foot. So we sat on the sofa and I thought "I bet everything will be all right now" I thought "I bet dad will go away back to Scotland and then I can go back to school again, because I'm all better from my flu now" I thought "I wonder if Tania Hodgsons cat had its kittens yet, I wonder if they were all tabbies like their mum?"

Jemima was being annoying like usual. She said "I don't want to watch robot wars, I want to watch the other side." I said "there isn't anything on the other side Jemima you big silly, its just the news" but it didn't work, she said "I want the clicker, I never get the clicker, its my turn." Jemima is terrible with the clicker, she just does it again and again really fast so you can't watch anything, so I said "you can't Jemima, you'll break it like you broke your new pink sunglasses."

That was when mum came in. She said "here's your treat lesonfon" which is what she calls us sometimes, it is "children" in French, she told us once. It was our supper, usually we can't eat it when we watch telly but she said "just this once" and it was hot dogs and oven chips which was a treat too, because mum says we can't have oven chips because their too expensive, their a real waste of money. Usually I would just be pleased by those treats, I would think "oh yes, how delicious" but this time I wasn't actually, which was because I noticed mums face. You see, all that smiling she got from getting the food from the supermarket was just gone away again, it was like it all went down the plug hole, she tried to smile when she said "heres your treat, lesonfon" but it didn't work, I saw it, she just looked all worried and desperate.

I looked at Jemima but she hadn't noticed, she was too busy watching robot wars and trying to eat her chips too quickly, she said "ow too hot" she is such a greedy guts. I thought "what will I do, I must help mum" I thought "but I really want these chips, if I don't stay and eat them then Jemima will steal them secritly, perhaps I should just stay and eat them really fast" but then I thought "no no, I must help mum now." Suddenly I had an idea. I said "Jemima I am going to the loo, you can have the clicker just until I get back" and she was really pleased of course, she said "oh yes" and grabed it right out of my hand. I said "I've counted all my chips really carefully, Jemima, if you eat even just one tiny one

4

then I'll notice and I'll put all your favorite dolls on a high shelf so you'll never get them again."

Mum was sitting in the kitchen. She jumped up a bit when she saw me, she said "Lawrence." I said "whats wrong mum?" and she went really quiet, she said "what dyou mean?" so I said "somethings gone wrong, I can see it in your face." She closed her eyes a bit, she said "oh Lawrence, I don't want to upsit you with all of this" and she sort of squinted her eyes. I thought "she will tell me now" so I said "all of what mum?" and she did a little moan, she said "I don't know what to do, its so awful, we just can't go on like this."

I really hated it when poor mum went sad like that. I thought "what can I do to help her?" but I couldn't think of anything, I tried and tried, I thought "this is bad" until suddenly I had an idea. So I said "why don't we go away for a bit, just until he's gone away, we could go to Uncle Harry's or somewhere." Uncle Harry lives in London, he has a big house. We went there for Christmas but it was just for lunch, we didn't stay because we are too noisy so aunt Clarissa gets a head ache, and mum gets worried Jemima will break Uncle Harries old plates which are stuck on the walls like pictures, they cost lots of money. But mum shook her head, she said "they're away, they've gone skiying." I thought "oh dam" I thought "there must be somewhere we can go" but it was hard actually, because mum doesn't know many people, usually its just us in the cottage. I thought "I'm not going to give up now when everythings going so well, when we got all that food." So I said "what about Grandma and Grandpa in Kew."

Mum shook her head again, she was blinking, she said "he'd just follow us . . ." But then she stopped, she frowned like she was thinking really hard, and she said "unless . . ." This was good, at least she wasn't just saying "no, nothing will work" so I said "unless what?" And then she said it, she said "unless we went somewhere really far away. Somewhere he'd never be able to find us. Somewhere like Rome." Now she sort of squinted like this was better and better and she said "actually we could you know. I've got our passports from that time we almost went to France."

This was different, this was a big surprise. Mum sometimes talked about Rome where she lived years ago before I was born, and how we must all go one day to see the fountains which were so beautifull and eat the food which was so delicious, but I never thought it would happen, especially suddenly like this. Another surprise was that mum didn't look so worreid anymore, in fact she even did a little tiny smile, that was good. I didn't want to stop mums new smile of course, I really wanted it to stay, but I just didn't know, I couldn't help it. So I said "but what about school?" because I had tests at the end of term, you see, and I had my science project too, I was doing SPACE for Mr Simmons, who was my favorite teacher. But Mum didn't mind, that was good too, she didn't go sad after all. She said "we could take all your books so I can teach you for your tests and help with your project. And anyway it wouldn't be for very long, just till we are sure dads gone away. I could ring the school and say you've still got the flu."

I thought "I suppose so, if its just for a short time. I can take my book on Space that I got for Christmas from Uncle Harry and Aunt Clarissa, that will be for my science project." I thought "it'll be a shame if I miss Tania Hodgsons kittens" but then I thought "it will be nice to see the lovely fountains." But then before I could think anything else the door pushed open with a bang and Jemima came in and said "robot wars finished." Probably she guessed we were talking about something without her, she had her spying look so I bet she was listening at the key hole but she couldn't hear anything. You have to watch Jemima because she is everywhere. Mum pretended she wasn't surprised, she pretended she was expecting her to come in suddenly like that, she clapped her hands in the air like she had a special treat and said "Jemima, we've got some big, big news. We're thinking of going away."

I thought "I will help mum" so I said "Yes, isn't it exciting, we are going to Rome, won't that be nice." I don't think Jemima knew anything about rome really, but she made her silly surprised face to pretend she did, then she clapped her hands and shouted "oh yes Rome Rome".

So suddenly it was a real plan now, it was all finished. Mum was so pleased, she was smiling and smiling, that was good, that was wonderfull, because she hardly did that for weeks, not since I got the flu and dad came down from scotland secretly. It was like it was bubbeling out of her and making her eyes go blink blink. I thought "oh hurrah" I thought "this is good" I thought "I hope it doesn't all just go away again."

I went back and ate my hot dogs and Jemima didn't eat lots of my chips after all, she might have got one or two, it was hard to tell. Then mum said there was no point in dillidallying, we must go to Rome right now, we must go tommorrow morning, which meant we had to start packing straight away. She said we had to be very careful, we mustn't take too many things because they wouldn't fit in the car, so she gave me and Jemima three boxes each. Jemima talked to all her dolls and her animals, she said "are you going to be good, no, then you can't come" or "all right then, you can come to Rome" then she threw them into her boxes with some other things all in a rush, and she didn't take any notise when I told her "Jemima you must chose carefully or you'll leave your favorite things behind and then you'll cry," she just got angry and shouted "but I have been careful, I won't cry."

I thought "wow, we are going to Rome, that's amazing." It wasn't easy packing. I wanted to take my computer consel, my football game, my drawing paper and pencils, and also all my Tintin and Asterix books, all my lego, my hot wheels cars and track, my school books and my book on space and of course there was Hermann and his cage, but that was much too much for my three boxes, so I thought "uhoh, this will be hard." I could hear Mum in her bedroom packing, she wasn't keeping watch at all, sometimes she just forgets, so I thought "that's silly, mum" and I went into the sitting room so I could look.

It was a bit frightening actually, because when I started opening the curtain I thought "dads face might be right here on the other side of the window looking right at me." But there was a strange thing too, because d'you know a bit of me sort of hoped he would be there, that was funny. That bit wanted him to look in with his silly smile and his hair that goes up like smoke, it wanted him to say "hey there Larry hower you doing?" But then I squashed that bit, I blew it up, I thought "oh no you don't" and I thought "I don't like you dad, just go away, don't start pretend-

8

ing to be nice." But of course he wasn't there anyway, there wasn't anybody, it was just the window pane, all tall and black. I put my hand on it, it felt cold, and then I went right up close to the glass to look out, but it was really dark, the light just went a little way, it did a bit of the grass, there was some of a bush, and I could hear the wind making the trees move, swish swish swish.

After that I did my boxes. None of them were big enough for my school books and the tintin books together, so I took the biggest one, I cut its corners with scissors and then selotaped them round the books leaving gaps, though I had to put more selotape on the inside so it would not stick and wreck them. I was worried mum would get angry that I made the box bigger but she never did, but of course everything got so busy after that she probably never even noticed.

When I tried to pack my other things I found there wasn't enough room, Hermanns cage took up a whole box by itself, so I had to leave my football game, my Asterixes, and some lego behind, that was a real shame, but I thought "I like Tintin better than asterix anyway." Then I saw there was an empty space in one of Jemimas boxes, she was in bed now, so I put my Lego in there because otherwise that space would just go to waste. After that I cut lots of holes in Hermanns box so he could see out, but then I threw the box away completly, I thought "he doesn't need it, he will just have his cage" so it was late when I finished, but not really late, not dawn this time. I put the boxes downstairs, I put on my pijamas and brushed my teeth, four times each tooth like mum says, then I gave mum her kiss, she was still packing, she was smiling like before, and I went to bed.

When I woke it was just getting light and I could hear mum outside shouting "dam dam" so I knew something had gone wrong. I thought "uhoh, what now?" so I got dressed like a hurricain and ran downstairs without even brushing my teeth and it was cold downstairs because the front door was wide open. Mum was standing by the car, there were some bags already in it and lots more on the ground. She said "dam this car" and her smile was all gone now just like I thought, she looked tired and scared and she said "I just cant get everything in." Then she looked all round and suddenly she shouted "I don't care if your out there."

Though I hadn't even had my breakfast I thought "I will help, I will make her all right again" so I said "don't worry mum, I'm sure they'll all go in" and I helped her try the bags in different ways, but they just wouldn't fit at all, that was a shame. Mum was scratching her arm, it was all red again, and she said "oh god, we'll never get away, dad will come now, I just know he will."

That was when a funny thing happened. When she said this I heard a car coming up the road, so suddenly I got really worrid, I thought "that's him, he went away to a shop or to eat his breakfast and now he's coming back in his car" I thought "I know I will pick up a big stick" but there wasn't one anywhere, that was bad. I thought "uhoh what will I do" but then when I looked up d'you know there wasn't any car after all. The road was just empty, there wasn't even any noise, which was really strange, because I was sure I heard it, it was like a mystery. So I thought "we're safe after all" and suddenly I felt much better, I thought "everything will be all right now." So I took mums hand to stop her scraching and I said "mum, we will just have to leave some things behind" and d'you know she got better too, she said "your right Lawrence, of course you are."

Mum is really clever, she can always help me with my home work, she makes funny jokes, she knows just what everybodies thinking, even strangers shes never met before, but sometimes its like she just gets stuck and doesn't know what to do next, so I have to help her and give her a little push. I was worried she would say I must leave one of my three boxes behind but it was all right, she took one of hers instead. It had the big silver candel stick that we never used, some cups and other metal things, and she said "he can have it all, I don't give a dam" then she put it back into the house. Afterwards she took out two other boxes too, and when we tried again d'you know everything just fitted. I thought "hurrah now we are all right." I noticed she had put Hermann in his cage just beside my seat so I could look at him on the way, that was nice.

Now Mum got her smile back again and so did I, I thought "we will be fine now." We hurried back to the house, I brushed my teeth really quickly and then I made toast while Mum woke up Jemima and got her dressed. We were both in our nicest clothes which mum calls our Sunday Best, because mum said we must look nice for the passports man who would look at our passports when we went through the channell tunnell. Jemima ate her breakfest without making a big fuss which she does sometimes, she says "I want another egg" so that was good, and we washed up all the dishes really fast. But then, just when we were all ready to go suddenley she looked up and said in her wining voice "but I want to take my dolls house."

This was impossible of course, this was really stupid. Mum said "but you can't Jems love, the cars completely full" and I helped Mum, I said "Jemima, I told you yesterday you must think carfully about what you put in your boxes, remember, now stop being a big cry baby." But Jemima just isn't fair, instead of saying "oh yes you are right" she stuck her chin high in the air, thats always a bad sign, and she said "I'm not going without my dolls house, its my very favorite thing" which was just a lie, actually, because I hardly saw her play with it for weeks. Then she ran back into the kitchen and I thought "uhoh this is a disaster, I bet dad will come right now like mum said" and I almost said to Mum "maybe we should just leave her behind" but of course mum would just say "don't be silly."

Jemima is very hard to catch, she is fast and when you think you've got her she goes all squirmy and wriggles away and she bites. We caught her in the kitchen but she bit my hand and screamed right in my ear, so I could hardly hear anything for severel minutes and she got away. When she got away again in the living room, and then in the bathroom too, Mum blinked and scrached her arm and said "all right all right, Jemima, you win, we will take your dam dolls house." Straight away Jemima stopped running off and she came down the stairs quiet as a mouse with a special smile on her face that I hated, it was like she was thinking "ha ha I won again."

Actually Jemimas dolls house isn't very big, its a cottage just like ours, it was about the same size as one of her boxes, so I thought "we will just do a swap" but when we looked in the boot her boxes were stuck right underneath all the other things. Mum's voice went quiet and squeeky and she said "oh for christs sake. Look, I'm really sorry Lawrence but we just haven't got time to unpack everything again. We'll have to take out one of your boxes." I just couldn't believe it, I said "thats not fair." But Mum didn't take any notice, she said "Lawrence, I'm really sorry but I just can't be doing with this, we've got to go right now." After all the things I had done for mum, getting up fast like a hurrican to help her pack the car because she said "dam, dam" and helping her in every way, I just wanted to go far away, this was so unfair, I wanted to say "all right then I'm not coming either." But then something told me I could not do that, it was like a little voice. I thought "this is an emegency, dad might come any moment and mum is desperete" so though I was really really angry I didn't say anything, it was like I put all my anger in a little bag and did a knot.

I took out one of my boxes from the car trunk, it was the one with my hot wheels track and most of my cars and also my computer consel and my games, I took it because it was on the top, I thought "I don't care." Then I walked back in to the house and put it in my room and I got Jemimas dam dolls house, I carried it down and put it in the trunk instead. When I went past Jemima in her car seat I gave her a look and I said "I hope your happy now" but she didn't look sorry or cry or anything, she just kept kicking her feet and singing itsy bitsy spider. So I got into my own seat and I did up my seatbelt with a click. Mum came over and leaned down so her face was near mine and she said "I'm really sorry, Lawrence, I know that wasn't right but its an emergency. I tell you what, I'll get you a treat in Rome, something really special, how about that?" but I didn't say anything, I just sat very still and didn't even look at her, I thought "I don't like you mum."

Then I must have gone to sleep because suddenly I woke up, we were driving, Jemima was crying and mum was saying "but we can't stop, Jems love, we're on the motorway." What happened, you see, was that Jemima was sleeping too and then she peed in her car seat. I didn't say anything to her, because I still wasn't speaking to her, but I looked at Hermann who was going round in his wheel, and I told him "can you smell that nasty smell, Hermann, thats Jemimas pee." Finally we got to a Service Station, mum took off the car seats cover and put it in a plastic bag, she put a towel on instead, and she changed Jemimas tites and dress and said "poor lamikin." That meant Jemima wasn't in her sunday best any more, she was a real miss match, so I said to Hermann "I wonder if the passports man will let Jemima through now or if we will just have to leave her behind?" Then Jemima started crying and mum got cross and said "of course he'll let her through, don't upset your sister like that" which wasn't fair because I didn't actually, I was only talking to Hermann.

Mum got more petrol and got us some chocolate bars and sweets as a treat for the journey, and when I ate mine d'you know suddenly I didn't mind so much any more about the hot wheels track and even the computer consel, I thought "I was getting bored with my computer games, actually." I looked out of the window at the motorway, I watched to see that dad wasn't following us in his yellow car but he wasn't, and then it was like everything was new. I thought, "hurrah, we're going away" I thought "dad hasn't done anything really terreble after all and now we are safe in our car, driving off on an adventure to go all the way to Rome. Hurrah hurrah."

Eventually we got almost to the channel tunnel but then something bad happened. Just after we passed the sign for the tunnel suddenly mum said "oh god, I completely forgot, what about Hermann, he's not allowed." This was because of Rabbies you see, which is a disease they have in France and Europe, you get it when animals bite you, cats or dogs or rabbits, it makes you fome at the mouth and die. I thought "what can we do, this is a disaster, we can't leave him behind?" But then suddenly mum laughed a bit and she said "wait a minute, I've got it wrong, that's only the other way when we come back."

Even then I was still really worried. I said "what d'you mean, mum, we'll have to leave him in rome?" but she said "no no, don't you worry Lawrence love, it'll be fine, we'll get him a pets passport, its really easy nowadays, I heard all about it on the radio." I thought "oh thank goodness" but I was still a bit worrid, I thought "what if mum made a mistake" because she does sometimes, like when we were going to Edinburugh to see Dad and she went on the wrong road so we almost went to Glasgow instead, or when she left her hand bag in the library. Jemima was worried too, because she really likes Hermann, she always wants to change his water and give him his food though I won't let her of course, because she is just a baby, she would do it all wrong. She said "what if there isn't a pets passport" but mum said "don't be silly, lamikin, of course there will be."

We bought our tickets for the channell tunnell and we showed our passports to the passports man, who didn't mind about Jemimas clothes being miss matched, so we didn't have to leave her behind after all. We drove our car right onto a train, that was funny, and I put some coats on Hermanns cage so nobody would see him, just in case mum got it wrong, but I don't think anyone looked. After that we went through the tunnel and it was really quick, I thought it would take hours. At the other end we were in france, mum said I had been there once but it was years ago so I probably didnt remember, and I didn't actually. We stopped for lunch and I had chicken and chips, it was really delicious, and mum said "dyou know when I was in Rome I was almost in a film." I knew about that of course because she already told me lots of times. She met a man who was making a film about a lady who lives on an island in the War, and he wanted mum to be in it. She was going to be another lady who waves from a boat, but she couldn't because she was just about to come back to England with dad, because she met him there in Rome you see, so I said "yes mum, you already told me about that."

Then we drove on the french motorway for ages, we had supper at a Service Station and afterwards I went to sleep and dreamed I went to the cinema and saw mum in the film about the island in the war, we built a big fence to stop anybody getting on to the island and she had her sell phone to warn us if he was coming, so we were really safe. When I woke up it was dark and we were still on the motorway so I looked out of the window at France where everything was different, the houses had different rooves and windows and even the writing on the signs was different, with funny lines on top of the letters. I thought "I should tell mum that I woke up" but then I thought "no I won't, I will just stay awake secretly like this" so I just sat there and I didn't say a word. I looked up at the sky, there were some stars, so I looked at a black space in the middle and I thought "is that you, Great Attractor?" Jemima was off away in dreamland, Mum was driving, Hermann was going round and round in his wheel, and the car was making its engine noise but everything was really quiet. And d'you know it felt so nice, just us, driving in our car in france in the night.

Later I woke up, the car was stopped and mum was shaking me and saying "come on Lawrence, come on, Jemima, we're staying here." It was a hotel, it had big windows like the library, and I was so tired I just wanted to stay in my car seat, Jemima was too, she said "I just want to go home" but we went in in the end. Then it was funny because though I was so tired I couldn't sleep. So I lay in my bed, I listened to mums breatheing, I looked at the curtains, when a car went past light moved at the edges, it was like eyes going from side to side, and I worried about Hermanns pets passport. I thought "what if we get stopped by the passports man and he says "no, you'll have to leave him here in france, you'll have to give him to a pet shop."

Then I woke up again and everything was better. It was just getting light, mum was already in her clothes and she said "come on lesonfon we've got to make an early start." So we all got back in the car, we went on the motorway again until we stopped at a huge Service Station for breakfast, it was crussons. And suddenly I wasn't so worried about Hermann any more, I thought "Mum is really clever, she knows everything, I am sure she is right about the pets passport."

SPACE IS SO BIG. We are in the solar system, which is Earth, Mars, Venus etc etc. The solar system is in a galaxy that's called the Milky Way, which is really huge, it has a hundred and fifty billion stars in it and its a hundred thousand light years across. That means that even if you went at the speed of light, which is impossible actually because no space craft ever can, its too fast, only light can do that, it would still take a hundred thousand years to go across it. Mum says a hundred thousand years ago people were still just cave men.

But our galaxy is tiny really. Scientists say in the universe there are a hundred billion galaxies. So if you were standing on the edge of the Universe looking for our galaxy you'd never even find it, it would just be a speck. Scientists say the universe is spongey, the galaxies are in long strings and flat parts like paper hankercheaves, so it is like a big squashy net. In between the strings and flat bits there are holes, which are called voids, and actually most of the universe is just these holes, which are really enormous. A really big one is called Bootes void, which is two hundred and fifty million light years across. Mum says four hundred million years ago there were just fish and amphibians etc etc dinosaurs hadn't even started yet.

That means that if you thought "I know, I think I will take a lovely trip across Boots void" and you went at the speed of light, which nobody can, you would have to sit in your space craft from when there were just fish and amphibiens to right now, and all the time you'd never see anything because there's hardly anything there, just a few galaxies which would probably be miles away on the other side. All you'd see is maybe an atom every now and then, which would be so tiny that you wouldn't even notice it anyway, so I think it would get very boring. But in the whole universe Bootes Void is just tiny, it is like a little bubble, so you'd hardly ever see it. Its strange but sometimes thinking about the universe makes me feel funny, I want to hold on to something, like the table or a window sill, just so I won't drop up into space forever. Sometimes I don't like it, actually, I want to say "go away solar system, go away galaxies, go away universe, I don't want to know about how you go on forever." I want to say "why don't you just leave me alone."

After our crussons it was cloudy, and though mum played I spy with my little eye and who can see a red car first, Jemima said the towel on her seat felt lumpy, she said "I'm bored, I want to go home." Actually I felt bored too. I tried reading my Tintin but it made me feel car sick, so I asked mum "d'you think dad's gone back to Scotland yet?" Even when I was still saying it, when I was almost at the end, I thought "uhoh, this is a mistake, this is a disaster." I was right too, I could see from mum's face in the little mirror that she was really cross and Jemima was frowning like she was thinking "wait a minite, this is new, whats this?" She said "what d'you mean, where did dad go?" and though I tried to stop it, I said "he just went on one of his work trips, Jemima" it was too late, it was like Jemima guessed something was funny, because sometimes she just knows things even though she is still just a baby, she said "why can't we go home till dad's in Scotland?"

Mum said "don't be silly, lamikin, of course we can go back" but Jemima was frowning like she still wasn't sure, but then mum did a clever thing, she gave a little shreek and said "oh look over there, it's the alps." So we all looked, and up ahead there were mountains, they were white with snow and some were sharp like arrows, they were really lovely, I thought "I never saw anything like this except on television" I thought "we really have gone a long way now." Then I helped mum, I said "look Jemima aren't they amazing" and she said "oh yes they're just like christmas" so it worked, she forgot about what I said about dad.

After that the alps got nearer, it took ages, until there were mountains right beside the motorway, and I could see tiny houses high above us, so it was like they were almost in the sky. Suddenly we went into a tunnel that went on for hours, I think it was as long as the channell tunnel, and when we came out of the other end everything was completely different. It wasn't cloudy any more, the sun was shining, the sky was blue and all the bushes and trees and flowers and houses were lovely colors so it was like we were in a cartoon. All at once mum laughed really loudly and it was like she was singing, she said "hurrah hurrah, we are in Italy." That was funny, for several minutes we drove beside a big lake, I could see trees with long floppy leaves like dinosours might eat them, and we all shouted again and again "hurrah hurrah we are in Italy."

After that the mountains stopped and everything went flat as a board until mum pointed up ahead and said "look over there, it's an amusement park" and I saw there was a big wheel. I thought "it would be nice to go there but mums in a hurry, we will just go past" but I was wrong actually. Mum said "shall we have a go?" Sometimes she is like that, she makes everything fun like you are at a party. So we turned off the motorway, we paid the motor way tole, which you have to do in France and Italy, and we parked the car. Then I got worried, I said "what about Hermann, we can't just leave him" but mum said "don't worry, he'll be fine, Lawrence, we'll lock it." I wasn't sure, I thought "mum is really clever" and I watched to make sure she remembered to lock the car, the little stick things all went down, so I thought "I hope he's all right."

First we went on the big wheel and when I looked down I could see the car park but all the cars looked the same, they were all tiny, I couldn't see which was ours, and anyway I thought "I don't know what I'll do if I see a thief because I'll just be stuck up here, I can't get down." Jemima started crying, she said "I don't like it, its too high" but mum said "don't be a silly, Lamikin" and then she did a funny thing, she took Jemimas hands and sort of danced her round and round until she stopped crying and laughed. I didn't like this dancing, actually, because it made everything swing, so I thought "what if it just breaks off?" but mum noticed I was worried and then she danced me round too, and though I was still scared it was funny too, I laughed a bit, and nothing broke off in the end, we went down.

After that we went on the merry-go-round. Jemima said she wanted to go on her own horse, so I thought "oh good, I can go with mum" but then she changed her mind like she always does, that was annoying. We did the Coconut Shy and Jemimas balls didn't go anywhere near the coconut, so I said to mum "you shouldn't give her any, its just a big waste of money." But the good thing about the fairground was Mum talking in italian. First she talked it to the ticket man at the big wheel, then she did it to the merry-go-round woman and to the coconut man, and they all talked right back so it was just like mum always talked in italian every day. Jemima was so amazed she put on her silly surprised look, and I was amazed too. It was really funny to think mum had that italian in her all this time like some special secret.

When we went back to the car Hermann was fine just like Mum said, nobody stole him after all, so I gave him some fresh water and more nuts. When we started driving again me and Jemima made a hole between the bags on top of Hermann's cage and we invented a funny game. I pulled her hands and she pulled mine and then we let go suddenly and shouted "help help I'm falling." Jemima is annoying, she is such a silly baby, but sometimes she is all right. After lunch mum said "its still quite early, what d'you say we keep on going till we get to Tuscuny." I never heard of Tuscuny actually but now everything seemed exciting, I don't know why, so me and Jemima shouted "oh yes, hurrah hurrah, lets go to Tuscuny." But actually it took ages, it took hours and hours, so it was getting dark when Mum said "oh look, there's the sign, we are in Tuscuny" and by then Jemima was off away in dreamland and I was really bored of driving, so mum and me only shouted "hurrah we are in Tuscuny" a little bit.

After that mum said "we've all done so well today, let's spend a little money and have a treat" which was funny actually, because usually when mum talks about money she says we mustn't spend any. So we went off the motorway, we paid our tole and we followed a sign for an agro tourismo, which mum said means stay-

22

ing on a farm. It was a big house with a husband and a wife who helped us take things out of the car and laughed when they saw Hermann in his cage. Hugh Prowse at school says everyone is like an animal and if you want to know what animal it is you just have to think of the tail, so I decided the Wife was a giraffe, because she was tall and thin and watching everything, her tail would be like a little string. The Husband was slow and fat, he was a bear and had a round fluffy tail. Our room had pictures of mountains, mum gave us our baths and she said we must be good at dinner or we wouldn't get any food.

Of course Jemima wasn't good at all. She kept on getting off her chair again and again though mum said she mustn't, it was because she wanted to find the taby cat, though it ran away as soon as it saw her, I thought "I don't blame you taby cat." But luckily nobody minded, the giraffe Wife just smiled and said "kaybeller" which mum said means "how pretty." I was so tired that I could hardly eat my dinner even though it was really delicious, but later it was funny, because when I went to bed, even though I was really really tired, I just couldn't sleep. I think it was because I was too exited, because the day had been so amazing, the crussons for breakfast and alps and going to the amusement park. So I decided that this adventure of going to Rome to get away from dad was the best thing I ever had done.

ONE DAY SCIENTISTS got very excited because they found a moon, it is called Europa and it goes round the planet Jupiter. Europa is blue, it is covered with ice and it has lots of lines on it like vains.

But what made the Scientists so excited was that there is water under that ice, it is a whole ocean and it is lovely and warm like a bath because there are volcanoes. Scientists said "I bet theres life in that water, I bet there are animals."

Nobody knows what the animals might be. They might be tiny and boring like germs or they might be monsters, they might be huge like sharks or dinosaurs. Sientists want to send a space craft to see but its hard because Europa is so far away, and they will need a huge drill to get through the ice, because it is miles and miles thick.

Of course it might be a stupid mistake to send a space craft. When they drill through the ice the monsters might all escape and get onto the space craft and then come back to earth so there will be a disaster. Everyone will think they are safe, they will have their lunch and watch telly like usual and suddenly the monsters will rush out, they will destroy all the houses and shops and everything. But then sometimes I think "but what if the monsters are nice?" I think "then they must send a space craft really soon, actually" I think "or all the poor monsters will die."

The next morning something bad happened. I woke up and the sun was shining on a bit of wall really bright like summer, and I thought "hurrah today we will get to Rome." I thought "mum hasn't said I must get up yet so I will just lie here for a bit, its nice here in my bed." Then I heard a big thump which was Jemima of course, and she said "mummy mummy, look what I've got." I don't know what she'd got, I never found out, the night before she was playing with tiny shampoo bottles from the bathroom and mum took them away after she spilt one, perhaps it was one of those. But what was strange was that mum didn't answer, she didn't say anything at all. I thought "perhaps she is in the bathroom" but then I saw her shape under her doovay, so I thought "that's strange." Jemimas voice went all sort of squeeky and she said "mummy, whats wrong" so I got out of bed to see. That was funny, that was terrible, because I was standing right in front of mum, I was looking right at her and saying "what's wrong mum" but it was like she couldn't see me, it was like her eyes just weren't switched on properly, it was like they weren't looking at anything.

I had seen mum when she got worreid but I never saw her like this, this was worse. I said "mum, its time to get up, don't you want your breakfast" but she just talked really quietly so I could hardly hear, it was like she was yawning, she said "I think I'll just stay here, Lawrence, I'm a bit tired." I said "but you can't mum, we've got to go to Rome, remember" but she didn't say anything, she just lay in her bed looking up at the cieling with her eyes. I could feel my breathing going fast and Jemimas lips were going all wobbly like she would cry, she said "whats gone wrong with mummy" and I didn't know what to do, I thought "what about our breakfast?" I thought "I don't know where we get it, we can't go without mum" and suddenly I wanted to cry too. But then I thought of something, it was like I just notised it, I thought "I cant get upset too actually or there will be nobody left." I thought "I will have another go and this time I will make it into a game" so I said to Jemima "come on Jems we've got to make her get up" and I started tickling mums feet. That made Jemima laugh a bit so she tickelled her shoulders and even pulled her hair just a bit, we said "come on mum, come on, what about our breakfast?" But it still didn't work, that was a shame, she just pushed us away a bit and then rolled over, she was holding her face like she had a head ache.

After that Jemima looked desperate again, so I had a different idea. I gave her a serius look and said "Jemima what d'you think we should do now?" I wanted to stop her crying but actually I wanted to know too, I was intrested, because though she is still almost a baby Jemima does know things sometimes. It worked, she looked serious back, she didn't cry after all, and she said "I think we should leave her in bed like she wants and then she'll get better later."

I was really hungry now so I got dressed and went downstairs, and luckily the giraffe Wife spoke English when mum wasn't talking italian, and she said of course we could have breakfast in our room. She brought it on a tray, she did a long look at mum like she was worried, and it was really delicious, though mum hardly ate anything, just a biscuit, she didn't even finish it, and Jemima got blackcurrent jam on the sheet which means it is stained forever. After we finished I tried one more time, I said "ok mum, we've had our breakfast, lets go to Rome now" but she didn't say anything, she just closed her eyes. The wife came up and took away the tray, I think she didn't notice Jemimas blackcurrent stain, that was lucky, she looked at mum and said "you want a doctor" but mum said something to her in italian which made her go away.

Later she brought us soup for lunch, it was really delicous. In the afternoon I was nice, I let Jemima help me clean out Hermanns cage which I never do usually, I let her change his straw and clean his water bowl. Afterwards I read my Space book and I drew a picture of mum lying in bed, Mrs Pierce says I am very good at art and Mr Simmons says my writing is really excellent though I must buck up on my spelling.

Jemima played with her dolls house, I got it out of the car for her, but then she was really loud, it was like she did it on purpose to say "look, I've got my dolls house and you had to leave your hot wheels track and your computer consel behind, ha." That was annoying, I thought "how dare you after I let you clean Hermanns cage." She made her dolls have a tea party and she gave the dolls the glasses from the bathroom so I had to take them away, I said "you can't have those, Jemima, because glasses are dangerous." When she tried to hit me and she bit my arm I told mum, I said "you must put Jemima out in the corridor until she says sorry" but mum didn't do it, she didn't do anything, she just looked at the floor and said "please Lawrence love, I just can't do this today" and it was funny, I was sad like I wanted to cry and I was really cross, it was like I didn't know which to be.

The next morning when I woke up I thought "right mum, you have to be better now, you just have to" but when I went to look at her she was the same, she sort of put her arm over her eyes like she was hideing. This was worse actually, because now it was two days. I thought "what if she just stays like this forever, we'll be stuck here spending all our money." Suddenly I felt really serious, I thought "all right then." So I got up and I helped Jemima get dressed, we both went to the girafe Wife and made her bring our breakfest, and when we finished our crussons I started trying, I said "mum, we've got to go now so we can get to Rome and then go home, I've got my tests remember." When that didn't work I said "all right we will just stay here forever and spend all our money till theres none left." But that didn't work either, so I packed my boxes and Jemimas, I got the car keys and put everything in the car, and then I had another idea. I said "mum, we've got to go. What if dad finds us here." And d'you know this worked.

Though Mum still didn't look at me, she sort of blinked and then she sat up really slowly and picked up a tiny piece of crosson. It was funny, she hardly did anything, she didn't even talk but I knew, I thought "hurrah, everything will be fine now" and I was right. Though she was really slow and still talked in her yawn, she went into the bathroom and had a shower, then she got dressed, she packed her bag, Jemima and me helped, and we went downstairs where she paid the Giraffe Wife, who still looked worried even though I told her that everything was fine now, so that was silly of her. Then we got into the car and drove away, we did it.

The thing that finally got mum's smile back again was a sign beside the motorway, it said Roma 286. I saw it first and I said "look, Roma 286, that's not very far." I had watched all the signs in France you see, so I knew 286 didn't take so long. I looked at mum in the mirror when I said this and I noticed she smiled, and even though it was just a tiny tiny smile I thought "hurrah, mum is really getting better now."

After that I kept a careful look out and every time there was a sine I shouted "oh look Roma 253" or "look Roma 223" and each time I did it Mum's smile got just a little bigger, until d'you know she was watching for the signs too, so we would both say together "Roma 184" or "roma 139" and Jemima said it too but she was always after us because she still can't read, she was laughing and squeeking because mum was all better now. Then the car made a funny banging noise so Mum frowned and said "oh god, d'you think he's done something to the engine" but even then her smile didn't go away completely, actually she did a little laugh, she said "well he can't dam well stop us now, we're almost there" and then we realized it wasn't the engine at all, it was just Jemima playing with a pen, I don't know how she got it, she's not allowed pens because she will draw on anything, she is a wrecker, she was hitting it against her door.

The number on the signs got down to 56 when Jemima said "mummy mummy I have to pee." I told mum we should just go on because we were almost there, I said "tell her she can just pee in her pants, you can put her towel in a plastic bag" but mum said no, we must stop, so we went to the next Service Station, which was called Auto Grill and went over the motor way like a bridge. After Jemima finished her pee we were hungry so we all had pizza with ham and cheese, it was really delicious, and then mum said "I'd better ring Franseen" who was her friend from when she lived in Rome years ago before I was born.

So we went to buy a phone card, you had to break the corner off to make it work, and we went to the telephone. We had to wait for a man to stop using it and mum said "god, it's so long since I spoke to her, she's probably moved" but she hadn't after all, that was lucky. Mum started talking on the phone, sometimes it was in english and sometimes it was in Italian, and then she started crying, but I thought "its not sad this time its happy, her eyes look different." And I was right, actually, because after she finished she crouched down and gave me and Jemima a big hug, she said "I'm really sorry I was so down like that at the agro turismo, lesonfons, I really don't know what came over me, but everythings going to be all right now, I promise you, everythings going to be just fine."

Then something bad happened. We all went down and got in the car but when mum turned the car key there was nothing, there was no noise at all. She tried and tried but it was just the same untill she started getting all worried, I thought "oh no not again, just when everything was all right" she was scraching her arm and rubbing her face, she said "oh god this is a disaster, I told Franseen we'd be there by seven and we're still miles away."

Suddenly I didn't feel worried any more, I just felt really cross. After all I'd done, packing the car and getting us here and making mum get out of bed at the aggrotourismo I thought "how dare everything go wrong now when we're almost there" it just wasn't fair, I thought "dam dam, I'm not going to let it." So I undid my seat belt and opened my door and though mum tried to grab me, she said "where d'you think your going" I was too fast for her, I said "I'll do this mum don't worry." I ran to some cars getting petrol, mum was shouting but she couldn't come after me because she is always scared of leaving Jemima behind in case someone steals her, though I don't think anybody ever would actually, she is such a stupid cry baby.

I didn't know any italian of course so I did it in english, I said "excuse me but can you help us please, our car won't start." The first man gave me a smile but then he just went away, so did the second, who was a woman, and the third gave me a little tiny coin, it was brown, that was a suprise, I put it in my pocket. The fourth had a mustash and was climbing into a truck with a big picture of cheese, so I thought he would go away too, but then he stopped and climbed down after all, he said something in italian which I didn't undestand so I just pointed at the car, mum was waving and waving. He was called Ugo and he was a hipopoto-mus because he was quite fat with really fat arms but he was quiet, he hardly said anything, he had a little thin tail. Mum wasn't angry with me any more when Ugo talked to her in ital-ian and he tried the car key, she said "how clever of you Lawrence." But then her smile went away again because Ugo frowned, he looked under the hood but his frown got worse, he shut it again and shook his head, he said "non low sow" which mum said meant he didn't know why it didn't work, he said "kapoot" which meant it was broken.

This was bad. Mum looked desparate, she said "what on earth are we going to do, and we've got all this dam luggage too." I tried to think how I could help but I couldn't think of anything actually, all I could think of was "we need something really big to pull the car, like an elephant" which was just stupid really. But then mum and Ugo started talking in italian and all of a sudden mum was smiling again, so I thought "this is good, whats hap-pened?" and she said "Ugos a complete angel, he says he'll drive us all into Rome, isn't that wonderful." I said "what about all our things, what about Hermann" but Mum said "Ugo says he'll take it all."

Even then I was a bit worreid. When Ugo went to get his truck I said "we can't just leave the car here, what if someone steals it?" but mum laughed like this was the funniest joke she ever heard and she said "Lawrence love, whose going to steal a car that doesn't work, tell me that" and though Jemima got upset too because we were leaving our car behind, Ugo was already putting our things in his truck. So we all helped, even Jemima carried small things, I took Hermann of course, and though Ugo rolled his eyes sometimes like he was saying "you've got an awfull lot of things" he kept on putting it in till finally our car was completely empty. Mum locked it, all the sticks in the doors went down, I checked, we all climbed into the front of the truck, mum said it was all right just this once even though I didn't have a seat belt, and we went off.

When we were driving before it was like the numbers on the signs just wizzed down, but now that we were leaving our poor car behind us at Auto Grill they were really slow, it was like it took forever. Finally we were in a long road with lots of shops and buses so I thought "this is Rome, it isn't very nice" but later on I suddenly saw a big brown wall and mum got really exited, she said "there's the wall, Lawrence thats thousands of years old." I had never been to a town with a wall round it, especially a wall that was thousands of years old, so I thought "that's intresting." We drove through a big doorway, I noticed all the bricks were really thin like sandwiches and after that we went past big buildings with lots of flags on them, we went past a big fountain, and mum was pointing at everything and saying "you see that restaraunt I ate in there once, it was wonderful" or "I knew someone

32

who lived just down that street." Then she pointed at a big building with lots of windows and she was about to say something but then she stopped, so I thought "that's funny." I said "what's that mum?" and she gave a little laugh, she said "that's where I worked teaching english, actually thats where I first met your father" and it was funny thinking of mum and dad being here years ago.

The sun was almost gone down and everything was really orange, so I thought "I like this Rome actually." We went over a bridge over a river which mum said is called the Tiber, it is in a big trentch in the ground, and then Mum had to hurry up and look up the number of Franseens flat because Ugo said we were almost there. We stopped beneath a big building, mum went up and rang the bell and a moment later Franseen came out and she laughed when she saw we were in Ugo's truck with pictures of cheese. Franseen was from France, she had frizzy gray hair like cotton candy and she was a cat I decided, a nice cat, her tail was long and thin and white. She kissed all our cheeks and then when Ugo carried almost everything inside all by himself and when mum offered him money, an orange yuro note, and he waved his hand like he was hitting away a little fly and he said "no no" Franseen kissed him too.

The lift was really small, so we had to go up and down lots of times before we got everything there, and Franseens flat was really small too, we piled everything against the wall by the door so it was hard to walk past without making something fall off. But the first thing I thought was "look at all those pots" because there were tons, some were tiny and others were taller than Jemima, they were painted with patterns and Franseen said she

got them in africa. Mum said she was so sorry about all our luggage, we shouldn't have brought so much, she said "don't worry
we'll find a hotel right away." But Franseen said no no she was
sorry actually because her flat was so small, so it was like a whose
more sorry argument, she said she wished it was bigger so we
could stay for ages but we must stay tonight at least, she insisted,
and besides she had asked all mums old friends over for dinner. I
was pleased mum lost the whose more sorry argument, I thought
"thank goodness" because I was really tired now, I didn't want to
move all our things back down in the lift again, and I could smell
the supper cooking and it smelt really delicious.

Mum was excited when she heard all her old friends were coming and she said "you shouldn't, Franseen, really you shouldn't,
how lovely" she said "whose coming, I don't suppose you've asked
Beppo." I never heard of Beppo before, I thought "thats a funny
name" so I asked "whose Beppo" and mum said "just an old
friend" and I noticed Franseen made a face like she just ate something nasty by mistake like a beetle, so I thought "I don't think
Franseen cat likes this Bepo." She said "no I didn't I'm afraid, actually I havent seen him for years" and Jemima said "Beppo
Beppo, someone did a Beppo in his pants" so we all laughed, especially Franseen, she laughed so much that a bit of spit came
out of her mouth and she had to make it go away with her fingers.

After that Franseen said she wanted to hear all mums news,
every little bit, and she got out lots of snacks to eat. I thought
"those look nice" there was salami and pizzas that were tiny like
coins, but unfortunately I hardly ate any because we kept having
to get up again and again to stop Jemima from playing with the

34

pots, because she wanted to put them on top of each other or make them in to patterns. I thought "uhoh this will be a disaster, she will break them all and then Franseen will make us go to a hotel after all." Mum told her "lamikin please, I told you not to do that" but Jemima didn't listen, she never does, she just got cross and said "leave me alone" and though we tried putting them high up, it was impossible because the shelves already had lots of pots on them. Franseen said "don't worry, if she breaks them she breaks them" but then I had a good idea, I said "why don't we take the pots out of the bathroom, because there are just a few in there, and then we can just lock her in, that will stop her." But Mum didn't like it, she said "Lawrence, please" so I thought "you'll wish you lisened to me, mum, you just wait" and the doorbell rang.

This was the first of mums old friends who was called Gus, he was tall and thin and had funny hair like a big string which is called a pig tail, though he wasn't like a pig at all, I decided he was a dog with a ropey tail. Mum was really surprised to see him, she said "my god Gus, I never thought you'd still be here" but he just laughed and said "oh you know, the dolchay veeter" which mum said means having a lovely time. I think Gus was really hungry because when mum asked what he thought went wrong with our car he just said "I don't know cars" and he started eating all the tiny pizzas really fast till there were hardly any left, which mum always says we mustn't do because its bad mannars, so I thought "you are greedy, Gus dog."

Then there was a big crash, it was Jemima of course, I thought "I told you we should have just locked her in the bathroom" but none of the pots broke, that was a surprise. We were still trying to catch her when the doorbell rang again and this time it was Cloudio, Chintsier, and Gabrielley. Cloudio had a big woolly beard so he was a bear, he said "kara Hannah" to mum and then he kissed everyones cheek except Jemimas because she was still hiding under the bed. Chintsier was a nice squirrell, she was small with black hair that was really flat on her head like a cloth, she kissed everyone too. Mum said "Cloudio how wonderful to see you, you look really well, and Chintsier your prettier than ever" and she kissed Gabrielly so I thought "they really do a lot of kissing here." Gabrielly had eyes that looked sleepy like someone forgot to switch them on and though I tried I couldn't think what animal he was. He was just a bit bigger than Jemima, so I thought "that's the end of the pots then" but actually it wasn't, because mum did a clever thing. She got out Jemimas dolls house, which made Jemima come out from under the bed, and then they both played with it in the hall for ages, Gabrielley didn't mind that it was girley, that was lucky.

Suddenly I thought "what about poor Hermann, I forgot all about him, he must be really hungry" so I took the last tiny tiny pizza, I got it just before Gus did. I put the cage in the hall, which was the only space, and Hermann was in his nest, I think he was still frightened after getting carried by Ugo. I changed his water and put the pizza in his bowl in little bits and said "come on Hermann, dinners ready" but then I had to move the cage again because the doorbell rang and he was in the way, that was annoying. It was Crissy, who was the last freind, she had yellow hair that was short and went straight up from the top of her head so she was a chick. When she finished kissing everybody she said "you must be Lawrence and Jemima" and she gave me a hug so I thought "actually you are nice, I don't mind that I had to move Hermanns cage."

Franseen said dinner was ready, I could hardly wait I was so hungry. There weren't enough chairs, so Franseen sat on one that went round and round for computers, which was funny. I picked all the mushrooms out of my pasta because I don't like them, and then suddenly I had a funny thought, I thought "on Saturday I was just at home watching robot wars just like usual and I never thought that on Wednsday I would be thousands of miles away in Rome eating pasta." Mum looked so exited, her eyes went all sort of soft, so I thought "this is nice, I like sitting here with all mums friends from years ago." My favorites were Franseen and Cloudio bear, but I liked Crissy chick too, and Chintsier, and even Gus greedy dog, I thought "I like them all."

After the pasta Franseen brought chicken and potatos and more wine, I had fanta, which mum doesn't usually let me have, and suddenly they were all asking mum lots of questions one after the other. So mum told them about driving down to Rome and how our car was kapoot, she told them how we left dad's house in Scotland years ago when Jemima was still a baby when mum and dad got divorced, and about our cottage with its lovely view of the hill. I put Hermann on the floor in the corner, he was out of his nest now, so I gave him a piece of mushroom from my pasta but he didn't like it either. When I got back on my chair Crissy the chick said "so tell me, Lawrence, how long are you going to be with us in Rome?" and I didn't really think about it, I was thinking "what else can I give Hermann for his dinner" so I said "just a few days, until dad's gone away so its safe again, I've got my tests at the end of term." But it was a mistake of course, I got it wrong again, that was stupid, because when I looked up Franseen was giving me a funny look and she said "what d'you mean until its safe again?"

I thought "what will I say now?" and Jemima was looking at me with her mouth open full of chewed pasta, so I thought "I hope mum will say something clever like she did with the alps" but d'you know she forgot too, that was strange. She never forgets anything usually, but now she looked sad and she said "that's why we came here. Mikie came down from Scotland to the village, he was spying on us and he got in the house, he was turning our neighbors against us, it was just awful, I was scared to death he was going to do something to the children." Now they looked really shocked, they all started talking at the same time, Franseen said "but that's just dreadfull, I can hardly believe it, Mikie of all people" and Cloudio said "you told the police?" But I was looking at Jemima, I thought "hasn't anyone noticed?" because her mouth was opening wider and wider, you see, it was like someone hit her really hard but she wasn't crying straight away, she was getting ready. Mum said "I suppose I should have, but I just couldn't stay another moment, I just had to . . ." but she didn't finish of course because that was when Jemima went off, she was like an airaid siren, you couldn't hear a thing. I thought "uhoh" I thought "it wasn't just me this time, mum did it worse actually."

Mum looked like a bee stung her, she turned to Jemima, who

was sitting beside her, and she said "lamikin, love" and she put her hands over her ears, though it was much too late, she should have done that ages ago. Jemima sort of choked a bit, she spat out her pasta and a bit went in Cloudios wine, I saw it, then she said "what d'you mean about dad, what dyou mean he was in the house" and mum gave her more fanta, she said "I was just being silly, I'm so sorry lamikin, I was just telling a stupid joke." Then all of the others started doing it too, they said "yes it was just a stupid joke" because though they didn't really know what was happening, they all just guessed I think, that was clever. Jemima looked round at them all, she drank some fanta, and she had a funny look like she wasn't sure, but she didn't say anything, I think it was because there were so many and they all said the same thing.

After that everything went quiet, I could hear everyones forks go "chink chink," and they all looked like they wanted to ask mum lots more questions but they didn't dare. Suddenly mum laughed and she looked strange so I couldn't tell what she would do now, if she would go happy or sad, I thought "I wonder which it will be" but it was happy, that was good. She said "its just so wonderful to be here with my friends again, my best friends in the whole world" and then she turned her head sort of sideways, so I wondered if she might cry a bit and didn't want everyone to see, and she said "I feel like I should never have left."

Now they all started talking at once again. Franseen said "its just so nice to have you here" and Crissy the chick said "why don't you come and stay at my place for a few days, Hannah, it'll be easy actually, because Hans has gone away to see some friends in

Sisily, he won't mind if you use his room." Mum laughed like Crissy was joking, but I could tell she was intrested, I could see it in her eyes. She said "that's really kind Crissy but I know we'd drive you mad in five minutes" but Crissy said "no, no, I just love children, and it would be so wonderful to really get to know Lawrence and Jemima."

After they all went home, Franseen and mum did the washing up, Jemima and me helped dry, we didn't break anything. We did the beds, Franseen said she would sleep on cushions from the sofa and mum said "no no we couldn't possibly take your bed" but actually there wasn't anywhere else, so we did. Mum and Jemima fell asleep really fast, I could hear them breatheing, but I couldn't sleep at all, I don't know why. I heard cars going past, sometimes there were bells ringing, and my thoughts went wirr wirr, they would not stop. I thought about our driving in the car and the Giraffe Wife and mum in the bed and breakfast with her yawn voice. Eventually I got bored of just lying there, so I got up and I went to the window. I could see people in another flat across the road, there was a party and they were all drinking wine. So I watched them for a bit and I thought "isn't this strange, isn't it funny" I thought "I wonder what Tommy Clarke and Ritchie Matthews and Mr Simmons at school would think if they knew I wasn't at home with the flu after all, but I was standing here looking out of the window at a party here in Rome."

CHAPTER TWO

Emperor Caligula was bald, he had hardly any hair on his head though his body was very hairy. He was worried people would laugh at him so one day he made a new law that said nobody could ever talk about goats, because goats were hairy like he was, and nobody could go up to a high place and look down on to his head, if anybody did they would get executed. Caligula could execute anyone, he didn't need to give them a trial or anything, when he walked down the street he could just point at somebody and say "I don't like them" and they would be executed, so everybody was frightened of him.

One day someone told emperor Caligula that he should fight a war, though he never had fought one before. Caligula said "all right." So he marched his army all the way to Germany and he had some fights there, but none of them were real, actually, they were just pretend, because Caligula was frightened he might get killed, so he made his own solders dress up like enemies and fought them so he knew he would be safe.

After that he marched his army to the English chanell opposite England. England was invaded by Julius Caeser years before but not properly, so Caligula could invade it all over again if he liked. He made his army go down to the beach, he got his arrow throwing machines and his rock throwing machines and he put them in a long line with their arrows and rocks all ready, and his solders wondered "what will he do now?" they thought "will he invade England?" Then suddenly Caligula shouted in a loud voice "I order you all to pick up seashells."

The solders thought "this is strange" they thought "why does he want us to do that?" but nobody said anything, because they were scared of him, they thought "we must be careful or he will get angry, he will do something really terrible, we don't know what he will do." So they obeyed, they picked up sea shells and put them in their helmets until they were full. When they finished Caligula said "well done soldiers, that is plunder from the ocean, it is ours, its a great victery." Then he gave them pieces of gold, and they all took it, they didn't say anything, they just kept quiet like everything was normal. So Caligula and his army marched all the way back to Rome to have a big party to celebrate.

In the morning I woke up and mum was gone, there was just Jemima, who was upsidown like usual, she is terrible when she sleeps because she goes round and round like a fire work, she is a kicker. I could hear mum's voice, she was talking in a funny way, I could not tell if she was laughing or crying, and I couldn't hear anybody else, just her, so I thought "uhoh, what now?" I jumped out of bed fast like a hurricaine and I went into the sitting room but actually it was all right, everything was fine, she was talking on the telephone, that's why it was just her, she was smiling. When she finished she said "that was Crissy, we're going to go and stay with her tonight."

Franseen was already gone, she went to work, but she had got us breakfast from a cafe downstairs, it was crussons and mine had chocolate in it, it was really delicious. Mum said Franseen left a book for me so I would know more about Rome, it was called Calamitous Caesaers and it was from a series called Hideous Histories. I already had one actually, it was about Henry The Eighth and it was really interesting, especially when Henry's cook tried to poisson him so Henry boiled him in his own pot. Then there was a thump because Jemima woke up, her crusson was called cremer and she got yellow cream all over her face, and when mum gave her her bath to clean it off I read some of Calamitous Cesears, I read about Emporer Caligula.

Then mum said "all right lesonfon, lets go and see Rome." Rome was different from anywhere I had ever seen before. Its streets are really narrow like alleys and they go round and round so its impossible to know where you are going, its like a maize and mum says even real romans get lost sometimes, though we only got lost two times. You have to be careful of the traffic, especially the motorbikes because they come round the corners really suddenly, they shouldn't be allowed, actually, they should be prohibited. When you hear one you must stop at once and stand still by the wall, so we had to catch Jemima lots of times. The houses are painted, most of them are orange and the paint is all stained, so I thought "they are old and dirty" but actually they are supposed to be like that, they are really beautiful and they are much nicer than houses in rainy old england which all look the same mum said.

First we went to see a square that is called the Piazer Navoner, it is long and thin because it was a stadium for races when it was ancient rome, but now there are just fountains. They are really famous, so we stopped by the biggest one for a bit to watch it dripping. Mum said "isnt it just wonderful here" she smiled so much it was like she might go "pop" so I thought "that's good, probably she won't go sad again now for ages." It had four statues of fat men sitting down, mum said they were rivers, I didn't really understand, one had his arm over his eyes like someone was going to throw an egg at him and mum said "theres an interesting story about that Lawrence" but she never told it in the end because then Jemima climbed over the railing which was so low it couldn't stop anyone, it couldn't stop a cat, they should have made it really high like a proper fence, so we had to catch her and stop her going into the fountain. I think she wanted to put her hand down the fish where all the fountain water goes down, it goes right down the fishes mouth which is like a big plug hole, so I thought "its lucky we got you Jemima or you might have fallen right down it and disappeared forever."

After that we went to another place called the Pantheon which has a huge hole in the roof, but it isn't broken at all, the ancient Romans made it like that on purpose and when it rains it all just falls right down and then it goes away through tiny holes in the floor, it's one of the most famous buildings in the world. We sat on a bench and when I looked up through the hole I could see birds flying, mum said they were seaguls because Rome is near the sea. I asked mum if Emporer Caligula ever came here and she said "he might have." I thought he would like it, actually, because nobody could go high up, there were just walls, so nobody could look down and see his bald head, he wouldn't have to execute anybody.

After lunch we went to the Forum where the ancient Romans used to go. Its all ruins, there are just a few colums and walls so I thought "this is boring" but actually that was wrong, you must close your eyes and use your imagination you see, you must think " thousands of years ago it was all brand new" because then it was full of temples and famous Romans, mum said "arent the trees wonderful, they are called umbrella pines because they look like umbrellas, you cant find those in rainy old england."

Mum said we would go to the Coliseum next, so I thought "oh yes hurrah" because that was where they had lots of gladiator fights, but then Jemima got annoying, she said "I don't like this road with its old stones, they're slippery" she said "I'm staying here." I tried to help, I said "come on Jemima, stop being such a big fat lazy" but it didn't work, she made her biting face and shook her fist at me. Mum looked tired, she said "all right lamikin, I'll carry you" so I thought "oh good, that's all right then." But then the queue was really long and when mum asked how much tickets cost she said it was better from the outside, she said "lets have an ice cream instead." I was annoyed, I said "I don't want an ice cream, I want to go in the Coliseum," but she got them anyway, mine was strawberry, so we all sat on a wall, and when I ate it I felt a bit better, actually, I didn't mind so much about the Coliseum after all.

After that something funny happened. Mum cleaned the ice cream off Jemimas face and she said "isn't it just amazing here, it's almost like summer, you'd never think it was still just march." Then she looked at us in a special way, so I thought "I bet shes going to say something serious" and I was right, she said "what would you say, lesonfon, if we stay on for a bit here? Perhaps until the summer?" Jemima laughed, she said "yes yes, lets stay" but I don't think she understood really, she just thought "if we stay then I can have more ice cream."

Mum looked at me. She was waiting. I was surprised actually, I didn't know, I thought "yes its nice here, the lovely weather and the delicious food and all the buildings and mums' friends." I said "but what about school, what about my tests?" Mum looked like she was thinking and she said, "I can give them a ring. I'm sure they wont mind if you take a bit of time off, after all you'll be learning lots here, you will be learning about Rome. For that matter you could even go to school here." That made me laugh, I said "but how can I mum, don't be silly, I don't speak italian" but mum said "you can learn some, I can teach you." I wasn't sure, I thought "I bet it will be hard, it will take ages" but then I thought "if mum says they wont mind about the tests she must know." I thought "she's not sad here, thats good" I thought "dad won't ever find us in Rome, and we won't have to worry about Hermanns pets passport yet, that's good too" so I said "all right then mum, lets stay."

Mum was so pleased she gave me a big hug and then she gave Jemima one too when Jemima pushed in. After that mum looked serious again and she said "not that it'll be easy. I'll need to earn some money, Rome's dreadfull for that sort of thing, and of course we'll need somewhere to live" but then she laughed, she said "who knows maybe I'll meet that film director again and he'll put me in some film, but no, he'll be in Holywood by now, or he'll be working as a waiter in some restaurant, that's more likely" and I thought "that would be nice, if mum was in a film, we could all go to the cinema and see her."

On the bus going back mum started teaching us italian, she pointed at things out of the window and I learned "keyazer" which means "church" and "makiner" which means "car" and "pizza" which means "pizza" so I thought "this is quite easy, actually, perhaps I can learn italian after all." When we got back mum told Franseen we were going to stay till the summer and Franseen gave a look like she was surprised, she said "but that's wonderful news."

We couldn't go to Crissy chicks yet because she was still at work, so Franseen said "just sit down and relax, have a glass of wine" and mum said "oh thank you, what would you like, Lawrence, red wine or white?" which made me laugh because I don't like wine of course, I just drink juice. Then Franseen started asking mum all about dad, so I thought "uhoh, be carefull, don't forget Jemima." She wasn't doing the pots this time, that was lucky, she was watching telly in italian instead, there was a man with a tiny beard asking questions and some ladies standing in a line just wearing their underpants, but she was listening to us, I could tell, her eyes looked round at us sometimes, so I thought "don't make her go off like an airaid siren again."

But it was all right, mum just said things she already said lots of times, how she and dad didn't see eyetoeye, he was always going away on his work trips, she was lonely in Scotland and dad always wanted her to visit his reletives. Franseen said "you were from different worlds" which was funny, I thought "what d'you mean Franseen cat, dad is from space?" Mum said it was all right when she and dad were in Rome, she said she really tried to be friends with his reletives but they never liked her, they thought she was stuckup, though actually I really like uncle Kevin and auntie Susie and my cousins Robbie Charlie and Alice. It was always nice seeing them when we went up to stay with dad for his weekends, even though they laughed at how I had an english accent now. They live in a big house in Glasgow, uncle Kevin is a plummer and he has his own company, uncle Harry in London says plumming is not a profession its just a job, but they are nice, cousin Robbie has a really good computer, we played Flying Ace, Asasins and Nortilus Ned.

Then Franseen went and checked on Jemima because she wasn't watching the telly any more, she was lying flat on the sofer now and her eyes were closed, I thought "I bet shes just pretending" but then she snored a bit too. Franseen came back and now she talked to mum in a wisper, so I thought "she's being careful, that's good" she said "and then he comes down and frightens you at your home, that's so terrible" and mum said "it really was" she said "you can't imagine, Franseen, he just wouldn't leave us alone, he got into the house and he told things to the niegbors to turn them against us, I was so scared for the children, it was just awful."

Franseen did blinks with her eyes, it was in a funny way like she wasn't sure, and she said "but Mikie of all people, I can hardly believe it, has this been going on for a long time?" Mum went a bit quiet, she said "I've felt it was coming for ages." Then Franseen looked like she still didn't understand, actually, she said "he always seemed so gentel" and I notised mum was frowning, she was getting annoyed, so I thought "I will help" and I said "he was all right before, when we went up to Scotland for our week-ends, he bought us treats and took us to the zoo, but that wasn't real actually you see, because he was just pretending to be nice."

Franseen shook her head, she said "what did he do, did he hurt any of you?" Mum was giving her a look now, she was holding her arm with her hand like she wanted to really scrach it, I saw it, so I thought "that's enough asking lots of questions, Franseen, don't make mum get upset now when she's all cheerful again." Mum said "I didn't let him." I thought "I know, I will stop this, I will interupt" so I said "actually I'm really thirsty, Franseen, can I have a glass of water please?" but it didn't work. Franseen got up and got me the glass of water but then she just went on, that was stupid, she said "did the police come?" Now Mums voice started going different, I heard it, it was like a sort of growel, she said "there would have been no point, he'd have just turned them against us, he could fool anyone" and she gave Franseen a funny look, she said "we just had to get away."

I thought "uhoh, something will happen now" but it didn't, actually. They both just sat there, Franseen was frowning and

49

sqinting her eyes like it was too sunny, which was silly because we were all inside, and mum was just looking down at the table so it was like she was reading a newspaper but there wasn't one of course, it was the table cloth. Then the telephone rang and it was Crissy saying she was back from work now so we could come over, that was good, and Mum said "we'd better go, can I ring for a taxi?"

So we woke up Jemima and started getting ready, and suddenly Franseen was really friendly, she was smiling and saying "I'm just so glad your all here" and I thought "I know what you are doing, you are trying to make us like you again after you made mum cross" I thought "but it wont work, I am still annoyed actually." She helped us take all the bags down in the lift, it took lots of goes. The taxi was big like a van, mum asked for it specially, and we had to move everything round to make it fit, but it all went in the end. I had Hermanns cage beside me on the seat and we were all ready to go at last when Franseen said "wait wait, just one second" and she ran back into the building. But she was much longer than one second, it was ages before she came back, which was stupid because you have to pay for a taxi even if its not driving, so I thought "I am really cross with you now Franseen cat, first you make poor mum anoyed and then you make us sit in this taxi so it costs more."

Finally she came back, she was breatheing fast from running, she leaned in through the window and said "I forgot to give you these." Jemima got a blue and purple furry monkey and I got another Hidious History, this one was called "Petrifying Popes." I thought "that's nice actually" so I wasn't cross with Franseen after all, I thought "I suppose you are quite a nice cat actually."

Mum kept on getting annoyed on the way to Crissys. First it was because we got stuck. We were in a road that was really narrow like an alley and a car just stopped right in front of us while a very old man walked to it from his house, and though he had a stick and a tiny lady to help him it took for ages, so each step seemed to take forever, untill mum said "oh for goodness sake, we haven't got all day, you know." After that she got annoyed when the taxi driver went the wrong way, she talked to him crossly in italian and made him go back, and she said he was trying to cheet us so we would have to pay more. Finally she got annoyed again when we were almost at Crissys, she lived in a place called Montyverdy and mum didn't like it, she said "I really don't know how she can live out here, its so boring." I thought it was nice, actually, because the buildings were all tall and new like Spiderman might jump off their rooves, but I didn't say anything, I kept quiet. When we got there I was worried mum would get annoyed with Crissy the chick too, but fortunatly she didn't. In fact when Crissy came down to the taxi they had a nice hug.

Crissy had a big lift so we got it all up in four goes. Her flat was white with pictures of ladies in old dresses and there were no pots this time, that was good, just some glass fishes in pretty colors which we put on a high up shelf right away. Crissy showed us Hanses room where we were staying, we stacked all our things up against the wall and then Crissy said "now come into the kichen and keep me company." She was banging pots and cutting up vegtables and she said "tonight I'm going to make you a real Roman dinner." Mum told her our news, she said "but don't worry Crissy we'll find our own place, you wont be stuck with us until the summer" and Crissy laughed, she said "I'd love to be stuck with you if Hans wasn't coming back. Oh Hannah that's really wonderful, it'll be so nice having you here again."

Then she looked nervous and she said "actually I've got news too, but don't think I should even tell you Hannah because you'll just laugh at me, I know you will. You see I've joined a church. There, your thinking oh how ridiculous. I knew I shouldn't have said anything, but its really wonderfull, its changed my whole life." Mum doesn't like going to church, we all went once for the School Birthday and she said the vicker was like a frog, she said he looked like he wanted to be on the telly, but she didn't say anything like that now, that was good, she just said "that's marvelous Crissy, I'm so glad your happy."

Then Crissy said "oh dam I forgot the onions" and mum said "don't worry we'll get some for you." So we all went down and we were almost at the shop when mum made a funny little noise, it was like she laughed or sneezed, I couldn't tell which, so I said "what's that"? and she said "I just can't believe shes gone all religious like that." I was suprised, I said "but you said you were glad she's happy" but mum said "shes not happy, Lawrence, she's a very unhappy person, that's why she's started this whole church thing."

I thought "that's a shame" I thought "I really like that chick" and then I thought "I wonder what will make her cheerful?" In the shop I saw a nice tin of biscuits with an airoplane on it so I said "why don't we get that as a present for Crissy?" but mum said "no, lets get her a nice bottle of wine" though it didn't seem nearly so good to me, actually. So when we got back and had the real Roman dinner I tried to remember to do all the things mum says I always forget. I did all my table mannars, I didn't just reach across the table and grab things, I said "could you pass the salt, please" and when Crissy drank all her water I noticed it and I said "would you like some more water?" Then I had another idea and I told her all about the amusement park we went to, I said "its near the alps and you can drive through a really long tunnel, you should go Crissy, theres a big wheel and a merry-go-round and a coconut shy, you'd have a really nice time, we could all go together" and Crissy said "what a nice thought" so I thought "that's good, that will help."

Then mum started getting excited, I could see it in her face, she said "I'm so out of touch with rome, tell me all the latest, whats it like finding a flat, are there any jobs out there?" I wasn't sure about that actually. In England mum read books and wrote her reports which she does at home, I thought "what if she gets a job here like dad, what if she has to go on worktrips, she can't just leave us behind." But then I noticed Crissy didn't look exited back, she just looked serious, I thought "mum won't like this" and I was right. Crissy said "everythings really hard here these days, Hannah" she said there weren't many jobs, especially for foriegners, so I thought "oh good" and she said flats were really expensive, anything cheap was a really long way from the center. That made mum get cross, she said "but we have to be in the center, that's the whole point, thats Rome." I thought "if we can't find a flat then I suppose we'll just have to go home" I thought "then I can do my tests after all" but then I thought "but mum might go sad again, at least she's cheerful here" so I didn't know what I thought any more.

THE NEXT MORNING when we ate our breakfast Crissy was really cheerful so I thought "thats good" I thought "I bet it helped that I remembered my table mannars and told her about the amusement park." She said "I don't want to go on and on about my church" but then she talked about it for ages actually, it was like she couldn't stop, it just bubbeled right out of her. She said that when she got lost she asked Jesus, it was like she could ring him on a special telephone and he told her which way to go. I thought "that's intresting" so I told her how we got lost twice yesterday because the streets went round and round, and then I told her how we looked in mums guide book which had maps at the back, so we always found our way in the end, I said "you should get one like that."

Crissy smiled, she gave me her special eyes wide open look, she does that sometimes, and then she said to mum "will you be here for dinner tonight? Your probably too tired, you've only just got here, but you see I was thinking of asking some of my new friends over, they'd so like to meet you." Mum said "Of course Crissy that would be really lovely" but afterwards when we went down in the lift she said "god I hope she's not trying to convert us" which she said meant making us go to her church.

Mum said we must try and find a flat now, so she bought a magazine called porter portaisy and then we went to a café. We

54

all sat on stools, even Jemima, though her feet were miles off the ground, so I thought "I bet you fall off" it was because mum said it cost more if you sit down at a table. Jemima got a glass pot of sugar and she started pouring the sugar in a little mountain, so I thought "now there will be trouble" but actually Mum didn't see because she was too busy reading her porter portaisey, she said "god Crissies right, I just can't believe these prices" and though I knew I should tell her about the sugar it was really funny watching and I wanted to see how big the mountain would get, so I just kept quiet.

Soon Jemima finished the whole pot, her mountain was so big now that some was spilling on to the floor, she reached for another pot but it was too far, and mum said "wait a minute, that looks nice. It's still a lot more than I was thinking of but its not that bad, its better than all the others, and it would be so amazing to be in Trasteveray, I bet its already gone." Then suddenley she was in a real hurry, she got up from her stool and said "come on lesonfon, lets give them a ring" and I thought "watch out now Jemima, you just wait" but d'you know mum never even noticed the mountain. I think she was too excited about her flat, you see, she lifted Jemima off her stool and Jemima didn't say anything of course, she just smiled like she was thinking "ha ha." So we went out into the road, we left the mountain behind, and I couldn't tell mum about it now because it was too late, she would say "why didn't you tell me before" and I would get blamed. So she never ever knew about that mountain at all, that is strange. I think about it sometimes, actually, and it makes me a bit sad. I think "now its too late."

We went to a telephone in the street, mum talked in italian and she got a big smile, she said "we've got an appointment, isnt that fantastic" and I thought "oh yes that's good, if we live in a flat then we wont have to take all our things up and down in lifts again and again every time." We took a tram, I never went on one before and it is like a train that goes down the road, I learned "gato" which is "cat" and "carnay " which is "dog" and "pigiony" which is "pigion." Then mum got up from her seat really quickly and she said "actually lets get out here, we've got ages." I thought "I wonder what it is, is there some treat, is there a zoo?" but it wasn't that at all. Mum took us down a couple of streets and then she pointed up at a high building, her eyes went sort of dreamy, and she said "you see those windows, I used to live up there with Crissy and another girl, that was such a nice time."

I thought "when mum lived there I wasn't here, I wasn't any-where actually, she didn't even know about me." That was strange, it was like I couldn't think it, I just couldn't. Actually I felt a bit cross with mum for being here having such a nice time without me, so I didn't want to look at the window, I thought "there are too many so I can't see which it is." I said "what about the flat, we'll be late, we'll miss it mum" but she said "there's still lots of time. I know, lesonfon, lets go to the bar, that's where I always went for my morning coffee."

So we went to the bar, mum squinted her eyes at the lady like it was really sunny and she said "Clarer say too?" which means "Clarer is it you?" and the lady squinted up her eyes as well, but she said no, she wasn't Clarer, actually, she was Jeener, she didn't know about Clarer, so I said "then lets go and see the flat then mum" but mum said "no, lets stay here anyway and have a drink" she said "lets sit outside" though it was stupid actually because it meant we had to pay more, and of course that was what made everything go all wrong.

Mum sat in her chair, it was a lovely sunny day, we were all sitting side by side in a line looking at the square, there was a market and people were buying vegtables, and she said "I just loved living round here, it's a real neyberhood" and I said "I don't like this apple juice, its nasty" I said "can I try some of yours Jemima?" She had blackcurrent you see, I never had that one before, and actually mum shouldn't have given it to her, because she would stain everything forever. Jemima didn't say anything, so I said "Jemima you have to share remember" but she just made a sucking noise with her straw, so I thought "that's rude, that's not good mannars." I looked at mum but she was just leaning back on her chair with her eyes closed, so I thought "all right then."

I was quick, I leaned over and got Jemimas bottle from her, it was just to make her share, because mum says we always must. But Jemima was bad, she did a shriek and she tried to grab it back though I hadn't even got any yet, I was still just getting it to my mouth. Then mum said "Lawrence for goodness sake," which wasn't fair so I said "I just want to try a bit" and I didn't let go, we were both holding it, you see. I said "she has to share" and then when mum said "let go Lawrence" there was an accident, it wasn't my fault, it just sort of jumped, it happened by itself, and it went all over Jemimas shirt with rabbits, so I thought "uhoh, thats stained forever then."

Mum gave me a really cross look, which wasn't fair either be-

57

cause I hadn't done anything wrong, it was Jemimas fault, I asked her nicely, and then mum reached down under her chair. I think she wanted to get a paper hankercheif to wipe Jemima's shirt with rabbits but I don't know actually, because she never got it of course, she just stood up really fast like she got stung by a big bee and she shouted "my bag, wheres my bag?"

It was her hand bag, she took it everywhere, so I thought "oh no, this is a disaster." Mum said "I put it under my chair, oh god, I can't believe I was so stupid, someone must have gone behind us and taken it." I helped, I got up and looked under all our chairs but it wasn't there at all, so I thought "I told you we shouldn't come here" but I didn't say anything, I thought "I won't upset mum." I said "was all your money in it?" and she said "no thank goodness, that's in my purse in my pocket" so I thought "that's lucky" but then she looked like she got stung all over again by another big bee and she said "my passport, oh god, I put it in there in case I had to show the flat people, oh god, I really can't believe this."

This was bad, mum was scraching her arm now, so I thought "I must help her or she will fall down into a big hole." Suddenly I really hated that theif, I wished we hadn't sat in a row because then I would have seen him, I would have shouted out really loudly and frightened him away, I would have run after him and got the police to put him in a jail forever, I would blow him up, I would do a Caligulla. I said "wait here mum, I will go and ask Jeener" so I ran into the bar really fast, but it didn't do any good, she didn't understand me because she could only speak italian, she just put up her hands like she was surendering and said "banyo?" which means loo.

Probably it was a mistake to leave mum alone, because when I went back Jemima looked scared, it was because mum was speaking faster and faster, she said "we're supposed to be at this flat in half an hour and now I haven't got any documents to show them" then she said "oh god and its Friday too, the embassy will be shut all weekend, I just don't believe this." She was squeezing her hair with her fingers and then she looked under the chairs again, though of course the bag still wasn't there, I thought "it won't just come back by its self mum." She said "I had all my makeup things in there, they cost a fortune, and there was Jemimas cup too, I just don't know what I'm going to do."

I didn't know either. I thought "what if she goes really sad again and stops talking like she went at the bed and breakfast" I thought "I don't know how to get back to Crissys, I don't even know which road goes back to the tram stop, and mums much too big and heavy for me to pull her up from her chair, we'll be stuck here all day." I thought "what will I do, I must do something" so I got some paper napkins from another table and I said "mum shall we wipe Jemima's shirt now?" but it didn't work, it was like mum didn't hear at all, she said, "I've had that bag for years, it was such a nice bag." So I said "I tell you what, I'll start wiping mum, and then you can come and help" but that didn't work either, Jemima pushed me away and her eyes were all funny like she was going to cry now, she said "I don't want you, I want mummy."

Then a funny thing happened. Suddenly I remembered a really bad day that happened ages ago. We had just got back to the cottage when mum remembered she left her bag somewhere, she didn't know where, and it had all her work in it writing reports about books, so she got really worried, she wanted to go back and look right away, but then another bad thing happened too, because she couldn't find her car keys. This was before she started getting all sad so she just looked serious and she said something really intresting, she said "one step at a time." So that's what we did. The first step was looking for the car keys, and eventually we found them, they were in the dolls box, which was because Jemima had got them, you see, she put them in that really stupid place. And then we did the second step, which was driving round and finding mum's bag, it was at the post office, actually, Mr Miller had got it safe, so mum said "there we are, everythings all right after all."

So now I said to mum "lets do it one step at a time. What is the first step, is it going to see the flat or the passport?" Mum looked at me, she was blinking in a funny way but at least she stopped squeezing her hair, she said "the passport I suppose. You have to have your documents or you can't do anything here, actually its against the law, they can put you in jail." So I said "all right then, lets go to the embassy, is it really far?" Mum shook her head and she said "we can get a taxi" but then all at once her voice went sort of wavy and she said "but we have to go to the police first and get a riport, it'll take ages, that sort of thing always does, and even if we get to the embassy on time, we're bound to miss the flat, someone else will get it, I know they will, oh god, we might never see another one as good as this."

I knew I had to think of something else now so I said "why don't we just ring them up again and ask if we can come later?" I wasn't sure if this would help actually, because someone else might come soon and get it, but d'you know it worked, that was good, mum stopped scratching and she said "I suppose we could try." She still had her phone card, she had it in her purse which was in her special inside pocket, I thought "I wish you put your passport in there too" so we rang the flat people and they said "oh yes of course, just come this afternoon." Then we went as fast as we could, we were almost running, mum carried Jemima on her sholders. We went to the police station and mum was right, it did take ages, a policeman with a really big hat did it all on a typewriter. But it wasn't too late, we got a taxi, we stopped at a machine so mum could get passport photos of herself, and then we went to the british embassy but it was still open, mum said "god, we just got here in time" so I thought "hurrah."

A VERY PETRIFYING POPE was called Stephen VI which meant he was the sixth Stephen. Stephen was really angry with another pope called Formosus. He came before Stephen, which meant he was already dead, but Stephen still really hated him, it was because their families were deadly enemies. One day Stephen said "Formosus shouldn't ever have been pope actually, he broke the law, so he has to have a trial." So Formosus had a trial which was famous, it was famously hidious, it was called the Synodus Horrenda.

They dug Formosus up. He had been buried for months so he was really horrible and smelly but Stephen didn't mind, he got his servants to dress him up in all his old pope clothes and put him in his big popes chair and then he said "now the trial will start." Lots of Romans came, they put on their Sunday best, it was because they were frightened I think, they were scared that Stephen would send them all to hell because he was friends with god.

Stephen shouted really loud, he shouted rude insults at Formosus, he said "you are so bad, you are so stupid, you shouldn't ever have been pope should you?" Then he said "come on, Formosus, say something, make God do a miracal" but Formosus didn't say anything because he was just a dead body. Stephen was really pleased, he said "look he lost" and all the Romans shouted "oh yes, he's gilty." So the trial was all finished and they took off all Formosuses popes clothes, they took him off his big popes chair and they put him in a big sack, they took him to the river Tibber, they did a big heave and they threw him in, then they all cheered. So the Romens never did say that it was strange to do a trial for a dead body, in fact they didn't say anything at all. But after, when they all went home to their houses, when they sat down and ate their dinner and it was really quiet, so they could hear their knives and forks go "clink clink" and the clock go "tick tock" then I think they all knew.

At the British Embassy we went to a room with lots of people sitting in chairs waiting and though mum wasn't scratching her arm any more she was still upset, she said "there aren't any numbers or anything, this is so stupid, how do we know when its our turn." But I had an idea, I thought "I will go and ask whose just arrived because they will be before us." So I asked several different people and they all said "no, its not me, I've been here for ages" and some of them were a bit cross, I think they thought I was trying to queue jump, until a lady heard me, she said "I think its us" and that was how we met the Vanhootens. She was Janiss Vanhooten who was the mother, she was quite fat with black hair and a nice smile, so she was a pretty pig, she would have a little pretty tail. She said to mum "so what happened to you?" and mum was still upset, she was blinking and looking at the floor so I thought "I wonder if she will answewer" but she did. She said "someone took my bag at a café" and then Janiss pretty pig said "oh that's awful, your whole bag, poor you, I don't even know what happened to my passport, isn't that awful, one moment it was in my pockit and then it was gone." She said "Its not a very good start, is it? You see we want to stay here for a year, we've just moved into a flat in Trasteveray."

That made mum intrested, she looked up from the floor and she said "thats where we want to live, in fact we're seeing a flat there this afternoon." So they looked at Janisses map, which was really big and noisy, people looked round and frowned, and Janiss said "its really close, we'd almost be nieghbors, you must come and see us." Then she wrote down her address and her telephone number on a piece of paper and she showed us all the other Vanhootens.

First there was Bill, who was the father, he wasn't english like Janiss, he was American, he was thin and old and he had a thin white beard so he was a goat, he said "nice to meet yer." The little daughter was called Leonora and she was three like Jemima but she hardly said anything, when Jemima said "mummy got her bag taken by a theif under the chair" she didn't answer at all, she just looked nervous, so she was a mouse. But the big daughter who was six and was called Tina was completely different, it was like she had got all Leonoras talking because she never stopped, she told us about Janisses passport getting stolen and her favorite food which was raviolies and how many dolls she had, so she was a bossy rabbit. I thought "I like these Vanhootins because they've made mum cheerful again." When Janiss finished talking to the passport lady and they were all going away because it was our turn now, Bill made his hand open and shut like a mouth and he said "see you round kids" which was funny too, I thought "mummy isn't a kid , she is old."

The passport lady said mum couldn't have a new passport till next week, but she gave us a peice of paper so we wouldn't get put in jail, and mum wasn't cross even though it cost lots of money, she said "god I hope I've got enough" but she did, she gave some blue yuro notes and a red one. Then we got a bus back to Trasteveray and after lunch we went to see the flat. When we got quite near mum started getting excited, I could see it, she pointed at cafes and shops and said "that looks nice" or "that would be handy" so I thought "I hope we can get this flat, I hope nobody else got it already because we went to the Embassy." We were late, that was Jemimas fault because she kept escaping on the stairs, there were lots as it was on the fourth floor, she giggeled and ran back down again and again until mum got fed up, she

64

said "all right, that's enough" and she just picked her up even though she screamed really loudly and said "I want to do it by myself." So I thought "uhoh, even if the flat hasn't been taken by somebody else, I bet they won't let us have it now because Jemima is so noisy" but actually it didn't matter of course, because the flat was so horreble.

The man who opened the door had hardly any hair, he was bald just like emporer Caligula, he was a sneaky dolphin, and he showed us round but it didn't take long because there was hardly any flat, the rooms were all tiny, they were much smaller than Hanses room. They were dirty too so Jemima, who had stopped shrieking now, said "I don't like it here, it has a nasty smell" and though sneaky dolphin kept pointing at things like a cuboard or a radiater, I think he was telling mum in italian how nice they were, mum was just blinking and not saying anything, so I knew "she doesn't like it either." I thought "uhoh, this will be bad."

I was right. When we went back downstairs she looked down at the ground and it was like the breathe went out of her. She closed her eyes and said "we should never have come here, this was so stupid, all I've done is waste money and wreck the car." Jemima was looking worried and I was thinking "oh no you don't mum" so I said "but its good we came here, mum, I really like it, it was nice seeing the Panthion and Piazzer Navoner and the lovely fountains." I said "I'm sure well find a nice flat, mum, we'll just have to look in porter portaisy again" but it was like she didn't hear, she just said "I'm such a fool."

Then I had an idea, I said "I know lets go and see the Van-hootins." Mum said "whats the point" but I said "they might know about a flat, you never know" and though mum said "they've only just got here" I told her "give me that peice of paper with their address, give me the guide book" and she did, she just did what I said, I think it was because she was sad. I tried to find their street on the map but it was hard, I don't really know maps and the streets all just went round and round like a big jumble. So I thought "uhoh what will I do?" then I thought "I know I will ask somebody." Mum was just standing there not looking at anything, it was like she was asleep or something, so I went in a bar and I asked the man, I showed the piece of paper, and he was nice, he pointed and talked in italian. So I said "come on" I took Jemimas hand and started pulling her, and though mum didn't say anything, she came too, and it was really near.

I thought "I hope those vanhootins are in, otherwise I don't know what I'll do" but fortunatly they were. Janniss pretty pig didn't look suprised to see us actually, it was almost like she expected us to come, she just said "hello again, how was the flat?" Mum started saying something but then she stopped, she put her hands over her eyes and she just started crying. She said "oh god, I'm so sorry Janiss, I'm not normally like this, its just been a really awful day" so I thought "uhoh, this is bad, what will that pretty pig do now, will she say go away?" but she didn't seem surprised by this either, that was funny, she just said "there there, Hannah, why don't you come in."

The vanhootins flat was really really huge, I thought "sneeky dolphins would fit into this tons and tons of times" and even mum stopped crying, she said "wow this is amazing." Janiss laughed and she said "It ought to be, its costing us enough." She took us into the kitchen where a lady called Manuela gave mum some wine and Jemima and me both got apple juice, they didn't have blackcurrent which I decided was my favorite now, that was a shame.

After that everything was better. Mum drank her wine and she told Janiss how sneaky dolphins flat was so horrible, and she got a bit more cheerful and even laughed a bit, she said "and it said in porter portaisey it was a charming pent house." Janniss showed us round, she showed us the bathrooms, there were three and one had a lady called Lara in it who was cleaning the sink. We saw Bill nice goat, who was in his studio, he didn't say hello because he was too busy painting, but he smiled and waved his hand sideways like he was wiping a tiny window, that was funny. I looked at the painting he was doing and I thought "I know that" because he was doing the Pantheon you see, but he colored in all the squares in the cieling blue like they were little windows, which was strange. Then we went to Tinas room where Leonora mouse and Tina bossy rabbit were playing dolls, and Tina told Jemima she could stay and play but she could only have one doll, it had a leg missing.

I didn't stay, it was too girley. I went down with mum and I found a book about animals which had a picture of a lizard sticking out his tounge, which was really long like a rope, and eating a fly. Manuella gave mum and Janiss more wine and I noticed mum was really cheerful now, she said "that's so kind of you Janiss, it really is, but I don't think we can afford that sort of thing just now" so I wondered "what's she talking about, what can't we afford?" Janiss said "oh don't worry about that, we'll be

67

doing it anyway, and actually it'd be nice for the girls to have someone else, they might take it more seriously" then she put her hand on mums arm and she said "really I'd like us to do this, Hannah, and anyway its no big thing, its only till easter."

I thought "is she saying we can live here?" I thought "theres lots of rooms so it would be easy, that would be good because I like these vanhootins apart from Tina bossy rabbit." Mum said "are you sure?" but Janiss pretty pig didn't answer, instead she looked at me and said "Lawrence, how would you like to come here and have some italian lessons with Tina and Leonora." I thought "so we won't be living here after all, that's a shame" but then I thought "but I suppose its about time I learned Italian" so I said "oh yes."

After that Tina and Leonora came down with Jemima, who had got two dolls now though she was only supposed to have the one with a leg missing, and then Bill goat came down as well, Manueller gave him and mum and Janiss more wine and they were all laughing. I finished the book on animals and then Janniss said "I do hope you'll stay for dinner" and mum started answering, I thought "she will say yes" but then suddenly she stopped and she hit her head with her hand a bit, she said "oh god, I completely forgot, the person we're staying with said she'd give us dinner." I thought, "oh dear" I thought "we forgot about poor Crissy."

So we went away in a big hurry, and as we went Janiss pretty pig said "just bring them over on Monday, siniora Morrows coming at eleven." Mum carried Jemima on her shoulders and we went almost running to the tram stop, but then we had to wait for ages for a tram, that was really bad. I thought "that poor chick, this won't make her more cheerful at all" and when we finally got one and we got out mum said "oh god its after eight now, I said we'd be back by seven" so I thought "I hope she won't be really annoyed with us" though actually it was hard to imagine Crissy ever getting really annoyed.

We went up in the lift, mum opened the door with her key and they were already all having their supper, they were eating olives and salami. Crissy got up, she was frowning but I notised it wasn't a cross frown, it was like she was sad so I thought "thats strange." She said "Hannah, theres been a bit of a surprise I'm afraid" and she pointed at a man sitting at the table, he was big with very short pail hair, he was a seal, and then he got up, he said "I'm Hans, so nice to meet you. Yes, I'm really sorry but my trip to Sisily got canceled, I didn't know you were all here, but don't worry, I can sleep on the sofa tonight" and Crissy said "I'm so sorry Hannah."

So I thought "that's why shes sad" I thought "uhoh, that means we'll have to take everything down in the lift again, I wonder where we'll go now?" I thought "mum will get upset now." But d'you know she didn't at all, that was a surprise, that was good. Actually she laughed, she just said "don't you worry, Crissie, we'll be fine." So I thought "perhaps everything is getting better, perhaps being here in Rome will make everything all right."

CHAPTER THREE

Scientists are very clever, just by looking through their telescopes they can tell how much a planet wieghs though its millions of miles away. Planet earth seems so big, it took days driving from england to Rome though we went really fast on the motorway, and places like Africa and Australia are much farther, they would take weeks. But earth is quite small, actually, thousands of earths would fit into planet Jupiter and millions would go into the sun.

But though scientists are clever, there is one thing they do not know at all. If you wiegh all the planets and stars and comets etc of the universe together they are just a small bit of the universes wieght, they are less than a twentieth. All the rest is a mystery, nobody knows what it is, its called dark matter. Some scientists think dark matter is just really tiny things that are much smaller than atoms, so they would make atoms look like mountains. They are called neutrinos or wimps and they are so small that they can go right through a wall or a car, they can go through people, in fact scientists say millions of them go through everybody everyday but nobody ever notices, it doesn't hurt at all.

Nobody has ever seen these Wimps yet because they are too small, so nobody is quite sure they even are there. I hope its them actually. Sometimes I think "what if the scientists are wrong, what if all that dark matter is really a huge black hole that nobody has notised?" It could be somewhere right at the other end of the universe or hidden behind a big galaxy. It would be like the Great Attracter but trillions and trillions of times bigger, so eventually all the stars and planets and comets will get pulled into it, it will take ages but nobody will be able to stop it, they will disappear forever.

When I woke up everybody was already in the kitchen, they were trying to find new people we could stay with now we had to leave Crissies, but they were not succesfull. Mum said "I wonder if Beppos still here, he might know of a place" she said "dyou have a phone book?" Crissy made a funny face, so I thought "you don't like this Beppo either" I thought "I don't like him too actually" but she gave mum the phone book. Mum found his telephone number but when she rang it he wasn't there after all, I thought "oh good" she just left a message on his answer phone, she said "everybodies probably gone away because its such a lovely weekend."

I thought "uhoh, I bet mum will go sad again now because we don't have anywhere to go" but she didn't at all, that was a surprise, she smiled and said "we can always stay in a hotel for a night or two." Actually Crissy chick looked sadder than mum,

71

she said "there must be somebody, if only I could think" and Hans looked sad too, he was standing in a corner with a funny smile like he hoped nobody was cross with him, he said "convents are cheaper than hotels and they are very clean."

Then a funny thing happened. I thought "I will be pleased because mum hasn't gone sad after all" I thought "I will be really happy now" but then I wasn't at all, that was strange. In fact it was the opposite, because suddenly I felt crosser than I had for ages, since before I got the flu and dad came down from Scotland secritly, it was like I was cross just because mum was fine now, I wanted to hit her really hard or I wanted to cry, it was like I didn't know which. In the end I didn't do either, I just said "I don't want to go to a stupid convent, I don't want to go and stay with other people, I just want to stay here" and Jemima was a copy cat, she said "I want to stay here too" so I thought "uhoh now they will think we are just a lot of cry babies." But I was wrong, actually, everybody was really nice. Crissy said "oh you poor things, this is just awful" and Hans seal said "I'll try my friends in Parioley, I'm sure they said someone was leaving soon" and even mum didn't get cross, she said "don't worry lesonfon, it'll only be for a day or two." So I felt a bit better, I thought "all right then" and I ate a piece of toast.

Mum rang a convent and they said yes, they had a room. Then Crissy said "why don't you leave some of your stuff here, that'll make things easier." So we divided all our lugguge all into things we would take and things we would leave behind, which was most of it. Mum said the convent didn't allow pets so we couldn't take Hermann, he was prohibited, we would have to leave him at Crissys, she said "I'm really sorry Lawrence love." I didn't like that at all, I thought "I don't want to leave him all by himself" but then Crissy said "don't worry Lawrence, I'll look after him, I'll take him in my bedroom each night so he's always got company" and that made me feel better. In the end I just took five tintins, a few hot wheels, my Space Book and my hideous histories that Franseen gave me. Then Jemima got upset, she said "I want my dolls house" and she started crying, so I almost said "you shouldn't have got it in the first place, Jemima, you should have just left it behind instead of making me take my box out of the trunk." But I didn't in the end, I thought "she will only cry more" so I said "we'll come back and get it soon."

At least it was easier getting it in the lift because we just had two bags now, it all went in one go. I ran up to the taxi really fast because mum said they just drive off if you don't get them quickly, I opened the door so it couldn't get away, and as we drove across Rome I thought "now I am all right, I am all better now."

The convent was like a hotel but with nuns. There was one standing at the desk and she had a nuns hat and big brown sunglasses which were seethrough so I could see her eyes. She gave us a long look like she was deciding what was dreadfull about us, something was really dreadfull, and when mum showed her the piece of paper from the British embassy she asked lots of suspicious questions, so she was a nasty panda. Finally she gave us our key and the floor was funny, it made all our shoes make noises, mine went "squeak squeak" mum's went "tap tap" and Jemimas just went "thump thump thump." Our room was all white, there was nothing in it except beds and a Jesus on the wall on a cross, he looked like he was rolling his eyes, so I thought "what are we going to do here, this will be boring, I havent even got most of my toys because I left them at Crissy chicks."

Mum put down her bag and she looked around the room and she said "but this is awful." I thought "yes it is" and I felt cross, I thought "you made us come here mum" so I said "its really awful." Then Jemima looked like she might cry again and she said "its really really awful." But now mum made a funny face and she said "no, lamikin, actually its really really really awful" which was funny so I laughed a bit even though I didn't mean to, because I still meant to be cross, I wasn't finished, but instead I said "no its not, mum, its really really really really awful" and then Jemima laughed a lot, she couldn't stop actually, it was like she would go "pop" and she said "no its, no its not, its really really really really really really really really really really awful." After that mum did a funny thing, she did a little clap with her hands and she said "you know what, lesonfon, lets escape." So we just went straight out again, mum said we mustn't run but we walked really really fast, I made my shoes go "squeak" as loud as I could, and when we went past the nasty pander nun we all giggeled.

Mum said we must do something fun now because the convent was so awful, so we took a bus to a big park which was called viller borgasey. We went on a machine that looked like a kind of car but it was a bicicle, it had four wheels and a floppy roof and me and mum did the peddling because Jemimas feet wouldn't reach, but it was hard so we went really slowly. After that we walked for miles and miles, mum said she was amazed how far we walked, and we ended up at the Piazzer navoner again with the lovely fountains and the fish plug hole. There was a toy shop there, in fact there were two, and mum said "you know lesonfon, you've been so good that I think you both deserve a treat." Jemima got a little green furry thing, I don't know if it was a dog or a cat, it was hard to tell, and I got an ancient roman. I wanted emporer Caligula but they didn't have one, the man looked quite surprised actually, and he said they just had Julius Caesear so I got him instead, but he was still really good, he had leaves on his head and was waving a sword.

By now it was dark, we were really hungry and mum said "lets go to a proper restaraunt this time, I know we shouldn't really, but to hell with it." I had spaggetty with bacon and eggs, it was called cabonarer, mum said it was like spaggetty breakfast and it was really delicious but it was a bit bad because when mum tried to pay her card didn't work, so the waiter gave her a funny look, I saw him. But then she did the other one which is blue, and that worked so it was all right. Afterwards when we left she saw a telephone beside the road and she said "I'd better ring Crissy, I promised I would" and then something really good happened. Mum started talking and suddenly she got a big smile and she said "but that's marvelous." When she finished I said "what is it, mum, is there a place we can stay, is it Hanses friends in Parioley" but she said "no, no, its much better than that, its Cloudio and Chintsier. Actually, Gus said we could come and stay with him too, but I think Cloudios will be nicer." So I thought "oh yes, that's really good, hurrah for Cloudio bear and Chintsier pretty squirrel and little Gabrielley no animal, hurrah hurrah."

Mum said we must stay at the convent tonight because we already gave the nuns her piece of paper from the embassy, but then we changed our minds. We went past the nun, it was a new one but she was just the same, she was a horrible panda too, and when we went into our room with its white walls and its Jesuz, mum made a funny face and she said "you know lesonfon lets just run away." So she rang Cloudio and Crissy and they said "oh yes come right now" and we took our bags, it was easy because we never unpacked them at all, and we went straight out. Mum had an argument with the nasty nun, mum said we must pay less because we weren't staying all night and she won in the end.

We got a taxi. Mum made it stop at Crissys and we went up and got Hermann and Jemimas dolls house, then mum quickly put some of my tintins and some of Jemimas dolls in a box so we had them too. After that the taxi went past all the old Roman buildings and they were lit up now so they looked really beutiful, mum said "isn't it just amazing" and we went to Cloudios. He lived in the suburbs so it took ages, I looked out of the window at the lamposts wizzing by and suddenly I felt really sleepy, I felt like nothing was real, that was funny. I looked up at the sky, I could see a big star and I thought "I'm not scared of you Black Holes, I'm not scared of you Boots Void and Great Attractor" I thought "here I am with mum and Jemima in a taxi going across Rome in the night" I thought "isnt it lovely."

EMPORER NERO WAS QUITE FAT, he had a beard and a really thick neck, so it was like his head was just stuck into his body like a tube. When he became emperor he decided "I know what I want to do now, this is what I always really wanted, I will become a famous singer."

He started right away. He got the best singers in ancient Rome to come to his palace and sing every night so he could copy them, and he practiced singing all the time, he never ate apples anymore because people said they were bad for singing, and every day he went to bed with a big piece of metal on his chest to make his breatheing stronger.

One day he decided "right, I am ready now" and he went to Naples to a big theater. There were thousands of people inside, they were all waiting, and Nero was really nervous, he thought "what if they don't like my singing, what if they all shout boo." He went up onto the stage and he started, he sang and sang for hours, and they didn't shout boo at all, every time he finished a song they all clapped and cheered. Nero was so pleased, he thought "hurrah, I really am a good singer" but actually it wasn't true, he was an awfull singer you see, his voice was horrible and rasping so nobody liked it at all, they only clapped because Neros servants secretly told them "you must clap really loudly or you will all be executed."

But Nero didn't know about that. He thought "now I will go and sing everywhere" so instead of going off and fighting a war like emporers usually did, he went to Greece instead, because Greece had lots of singing contests. Nero asked if he could have a try too and all the Greekes said "oh yes of course" and though he was really nervous, he won them all, every single one. He was so pleased, he thought "I really am the best singer in the world" but it was all a cheat really, his servants gave money to the other singers so they would sing really badly and they gave money to the judges too, they said "you have to make Nero win or you will be executed."

Nero was so happy, when he went back to Rome he had a triumph, which was funny because that was what generals did when they conqered a new country and Nero didn't conquer anything of course, all he did was sing. He had a huge procession, he went in a special carriage with big signs saying the singing prizes he won, and all the Romans came and stood beside the road and cheered and cheered, so Nero thought "they think I am wonderful." But that wasn't real either, because they were just pretending, they thought "he is a terreble singer" they thought "he is a really silly emporer."

After that Nero sang more and more, he just couldn't stop. When he started singing in a theater, people wanted to get away because he was so terrible but they couldn't, it was prohibited. Neros servants made solders lock all the doors so even if ladies started having a baby they couldn't leave, they had to stay and have the baby there and they had to do it really quietly so it wouldn't spoil Neros singing. Some people got so desperete to escape that they pretended to be dead so they would be taken out and buried.

A few times Neros friends and generals didn't clap and cheer him very much, they just forgot I think, and that made Nero really angry, he thought "whats wrong with you, don't you know I am the best singer in the world?" so he had them executed. But mostly when Nero asked people if he was a good singer everybody said "oh yes, you are really wonderfull, Nero, you are the best singer ever." It was only much later when there was a rebellion aganst Nero and everything was a disaster that people started saying "he's a terrible singer actually" and even then they were careful I think, they only said it quietly when he was in another room. So he never really knew, he always thought "I am just wonderful."

Cloudio was nice, he said "how would you like to go to a lake today Lawrence" and Chintsier pretty squirrell was nice too, she said "would you like some choclate serial for your breakfest?" so I thought Gabrielley would be nice too, but he wasn't at all, that was a surprise. Their flat was really small, it was full of books, they were everywhere like Franseens pots but Jemima didn't like them, that was lucky, she never tried to make them into patterns. We slept on a sofa bed in the sitting room which made my sholder ache, mum said sofa beds often do that, and there was only just space for Hermanns cage in the corner, so we had to put our bags and Jemimas dolls house in the hall and my box of tintins in the kitchen, and mum said "I wish I'd left it all at Crissys." The kitchen was small too, there was hardly enough room for us all to sit round the table and have our breakfast, and then when Gabrielley came in he started shouting crossly in italian and pointing at mum.

I thought "whats this?" I thought "thats not nice mannars, he's very rude." Cloudio and Chintsier both said "Gabrielley, no" which is the same in italian, but mum got up from her chair, which was what Gabrielley wanted you see, and she said "is that your chair Gabrielley, oh I'm sorry." I didn't say anything but I thought "don't give in, mum, that's your chair" but she did, she and Cloudio had a kind of argument, it was a whose being nicer argument and mum won, that was a shame, she drank her coffee standing up by the sink and she said "I've already finished my breakfast." So Gabrielly sat in her chair eating his serial like he was thinking "ha." I gave him a look when nobody was watching, I thought "that's why you haven't got an animal, Gabrielley, because you are a horrible cry baby."

Then something happened. There was a ring at the doorbell, Cloudio got up to answewer it and he did a big smile and said "I wonder who that is?" so I thought "I think you know about this person whose coming, they are your secret surprise" and I was right, because it was Franseen. She came in smiling like it was a big joke and she said "I've come to eat your breakfast." I thought "this is nice, this is good" but then I noticed mum. She said "how lovely" but it wasn't real actually, I could see it, because her eyes were really cross. Franseen noticed too I think, because suddenly she went quiet.

After that it got worse. Soon everybody was ready, we were all standing outside, and Franseen gave mum a little smiley look and she said "so who wants to come in my car? I warn you, you will have to listen to my music, today its motsart and motown, it will be loud." I looked at her car, which was new and blue, it was much better than Cloudios which was small and brown and had lots of scrapes on it, so I gave mum a look, it said "come on mum, lets go in her car." But it didn't work, mum put on her quick voice, it's the one she does when she gets cross, and she said "I think I'll go with Cloudio and Chintsier so I can catch up on all their news." I thought "that's silly mum" I thought "yes Franseen made you annoyed but shes nice now, and she gave me my hideous histories and Jemima her blue and purple monkey."

Suddenly I felt sad for that poor cat, so I thought "I know what I'll do" and I said "I'll come in your car Franseen" but it didn't work at all. Mum gave me a look, it was a really bad one too, that was a surprise, and she said "I think we'd better stay together Lawrence, in case someone gets lost." Suddenly everything went all quiet, that was bad. Franseen gave mum a funny look like she was saying "whats this then?" Cloudio was frowning at the ground like he was pretending he wasn't there and Chintsier was looking at everybody, her eyes were going side to side flicky flicky flick. But she was the one who stopped it being quiet, that was good, she said "I'll come with you Franseen, I really like motown" so I thought "thank you Chintsier."

Then it was all right except for Gabrielly. Chintsier wanted him to come with her, she started getting his car seat out of Cloudios car, but then he said no in his winey voice and nobody stopped him so he won, he came with us. He was in the back with mum and Jemima, who was on mum'slap, mum said it was all right just this once, and I was in the front with Cloudio. But mum never did catch up on all his news in the end, because every time she started talking Gabrielly just interupted, he was dreadfull, and then Jemima started interrupting too because she thought it was funny, she just shrieked, because she really liked Gabrielly even though he was just a stupid cry baby, which was silly of her. So Mum and Cloudio just talked a tiny bit in the end, first it was in Italian and then mum said in english "really, everythings fine. Its just so lovely to see you and Chintsier again" and he liked that, he did a big smile.

Lunch was pizzas, it was by the lake, you could see it over the fence if you stood on your chair. We had a long table and mum and Franseen were at different ends, so it didn't matter that they didn't talk to each other, because they couldn't anyway. Gabrielly didn't get cross either, but he looked round with cross eyes so I thought "I know what your doing Gabrielley no animal, your cross now just because you can't find anything to get cross about."

After lunch we went to see some ruins at a place called Chervettery, they were made by the Etruscans who mum said are really really old, they are even older than the Romans. The ruins are tombs, which are where you put dead bodies, and Cloudio said the Etruscans were really clever because they invented lots of things, they invented pesto which is a sauce you can put on your spaggetties, it is green, mum gave it to us once and I don't like it. The tombs were made of stone, they were huge and round so they looked like a whole lot of flying saucers. You could go into them down metal stairs but they were really steep so you had to be careful you didn't fall and smash your head open, mum picked up Jemima, she just grabbed her even though she screamed "but I want to go down by myself."

When we got to the bottom of one toomb Gabrielley ran round a corner and Jemima ran right after him. I thought "I bet theres trouble now" I thought "I will go and see" so I followed, and I was right too. You see, when I went round the corner Gabrielly was looking at something on the floor, it was a beetle I think, and Jemima ran up because she always has to do everything too, and she pushed Gabrielley a bit. It was just an accident, she is very clumsy, but it really annoyed Gabrielly so he pushed her back. Jemima just laughed, she thought "this is a funny game" but I thought "uhoh" I thought "watch it, Gabrielley no animal, don't you hurt my sister, she's mine."

He hadn't seen me yet because he was looking the other way, and I was getting near them when Jemima pushed him back again, I knew she would. Of course now Gabrielley got really cross, I knew that too, he didn't think it was a game, so he did something bad, he got her arm and he pinched it, and I think he did it really hard because Jemima jumped up really quick like she would cry now. I thought "right Gabrielley" I thought "I told you" and I did a funny thing. When he finally notised me it was too late, because I already got the bottom of his ear, you see, and then I just turned it round and round like it was clock work, I said "that serves you right, Gabrielly."

Even when I was still winding his ear I thought "uhoh, I bet something will happen now" I thought "perhaps I shouldn't have done his ear so much" but it was too late, and I was right, something did happen. First Gabrielly screamed and screamed like he was blown up, it was like someone broke all his arms and legs, which was really stupid because I only did his ear a bit, I thought "you silly cry baby" and then he ran back to his mummy and daddy shouting in italian. Next mum came round the corner, she was the first, she was sort of stamping her feet and she had her slit eyes so I thought "uhoh" so I said really quickly "it was Gabrielley mum, he started it, he hurt poor Jemima, he pinched her really hard."

But Jemima wasn't crying after all, that was stupid, that was bad, she was just sitting on the ground looking at that beetle so I thought "come on Jemima" I thought "you big stupid silly." But I didn't say that, I said in a nice voice "Jemima, Gabrielly pinched your arm just now didn't he?" She looked up but her eyes were all swiched off, so I thought "how dare you Jemima, I only did his ear for you" but then it was all right, she looked at mum and said "yes and it really hurt" and suddenly because she remembered her mouth started wobbling like she might cry after all.

Another good thing was that Cloudio and Chintsier and Franseen and Gabrielley came round the corner just then, so they heard her say it too. Now Cloudio started telling off Gabrielley in italian and mum told me off, it was a bit like the whose-being-nicer agument at breakfast. Mum said to me "how dare you hurt Gabrielly, he's only a little boy" but Cloudio shouted at Gabrielly in italian and he said to mum "Hannah, Gabrielley shouldn't have hurt Jemima either." Mum said "it still doesn't mean Lawrence was right to hurt Gabrielley" and Cloudio said "I know, but he was only looking after his little sister" so I thought "thank you Cloudio." Then they made us both say sorry and I was better, I did my sorry really quick but Gabrielley didn't want to say it at all, Cloudio had to wave his finger. I thought "that's all finished then, that wasn't too bad" but it wasn't finished, actually, because then I notised Chintsier gave me a really nasty look, so I thought "uhoh that squirrel really hates me now."

Then a funny thing happened. Franseen came up to me, she hadn't said anything until then so I suppose it was her turn now. She wasn't horrible, she said "better you don't hit the little ones, eh?" and then she gave me a little smile. But mum was standing right there and she looked really cross, she said "I've already talked to Lawrence, Franseen." After that it got worse, Franseen gave mum a slitty eye look and she said "what have I done, Hannah, why aren't you talking to me, why do you treat me like this?" I thought "uhoh, what will happen now, what will she say?" but it didn't go like I thought, actually, because mum did a big smile like it was so funny, and she said in a loud voice "I really don't know what your talking about." But that didn't work at all, because Franseen said "for goodness sake" and then they just looked at each other like their looks were ray guns. Suddenly I got annoyed, I said "stop it, this is just horrible" and d'you know it worked, they both looked at me like they were sorry.

Afterwards we all walked back through the tombs and mum walked really slowly so Cloudio and Chintsier and Gabrielly and Franseen got far ahead. I thought "uhoh, she will tell me off now, she has been waiting" but she didn't, she just did a quiet voice like she was tired. She said I must understand that it was hard for Gabrielley because we were staying in his tiny flat, she said I wouldn't find it easy if we had lots of people coming to stay in the cottage, how would I like it if they were sleeping in our sitting room so I couldn't watch the telly when I wanted. So I said "yes mum, I'm sorry" but secretly I was still pleased I did his ear. When we got to the cars he gave me a look, it was an "I'll get you, you just wait" look, but I didn't care. I gave him a look back and mine was better, it said "you can't do anything to me Gabrielley no animal, because you are too small, watch out or I will Calligula you."

POPE BONIFACE VIII WAS THE EIGHTH Boniface, he was tall, he had a loud voice, and when he became pope he decided "I am going to be the most petrifying pope ever." If anybody annoyed him he said "you'd better do what I say or I'll tell god and you'll go to hell" and it worked. Everybody was scared of him, he ordered around all the kings of England and France etc etc, he was like an emporer.

One day lots of his brothers and sisters and aunts and uncles came to visit him and said "Boniface, please help us, we don't have anywhere nice to live, we are desperate." Boniface thought "oh dear, I must help my poor relatives." So he got lots of land and cities, he bought them with his popes money or he sent his army to get them, and his relatives became princes and princesses, they had lovely palaces. But it wasn't enough, because there were more relatives who were still poor, they didn't have anywhere. Boniface thought "uhoh, theres hardly any land and cities left, what will I do?"

Then he had an idea. There was a very famous family called the Colonnas who were really rich because they had been pope lots of times, they had lots of land and cities, so Boniface thought "they will do." But when he started taking their places the Colonnas got angry, they said "you shouldn't be a pope, actually, Boniface, you cheated" so it was like when Pope Stephen dug up Formosus. Boniface got really angry too, he thought "I really hate these Colonnas, they have so many places and my poor relatives don't have anywhere, they have to carry all their things round in a big cart." He said "I will fight a war with you Colonnas and it won't be an ordinary war, actually, it will be a Crusade." This was funny because crusades were only supposed to be for invading Jeruselem, not for fighting Collonnas, but Boniface did it anyway, he told his soldiers "you can do anything now because you are crusaders, I promise you will go straight to heaven." So the solders fought lots of battles, they destroyed the Colonnas cities and they burnt their food and vegtables, they killed lots of enemies even if they werent Collonas but were just there by accident, until Boniface got all of the Collonnas places except one.

This was called Palestrina and it was really hard to get, it was impregnible because it was on a high mountain and it had huge walls, it was old and beautiful. Boniface got worried, he thought "how will I ever get Palestrina, this is impossible, it is a disaster" but then he had a good idea. He sent a messenger who told the Collonnas "if you give up, then Boniface will stop this war and give back all your cities and land." The Collonnas weren't sure, they thought "what if he is just playing a trick?" but then they thought "no he can't, he's pope, remember, Popes can't tell lies" so they opened the door and they all came out.

But this was a big mistake, actually, because Boniface thought "oh good, that worked" and he just laughed, he didn't give them anything back after all, he told his solders "put them in the dungeon." Suddenly a few Colonnas escaped, but Boniface didn't mind, he said "that's all right, I got most of them." Then he thought "now I will do something really petrifying" so he told his soldiers "I order you to destroy Palestrina, I don't care if its old and beautiful." The soldiers thought "all right, we will go to heaven anyway" so they knocked down all the impregnible walls and all the lovely buildings and it took ages, it was really hard work. When they finished Boniface thought "hurrah, now I have won."

But he forgot about something. It was the Colonnas who escaped. They went to see the king of France you see, because he didn't like Boniface either and they all made a clever plan. They got an army but it was special, it was tiny and secret, it went all across italy and nobody ever noticed, they thought "who are they, I don't know, they are probably just turists" so Boniface never knew.

One day Boniface was on holiday, he was in a lovely palace in the countryside, when suddenly there was a big crash, the door opened, and the secret army rushed in with their swords. Boniface thought "oh no, they have got me." But then a funny thing happened, because the secret army couldn't decide what to do. The Colonnas said "lets just kill him" but the others were scared, they said "but then we will get sent to hell." So they just stayed there for days shouting rude insults at Boniface until there was another crash, and this time it was Bonifaces solders, they came and rescued him.

Boniface went back to Rome, but he wasn't pettrifying any more, in fact now he was scared of everything. He sat in his palace and he thought "what if those Collonas come and get me again, what if there is another secret army?" and he was frightened of everybody, even the waiters who came to bring his breakfast, until he just died. After that the Collonas got all their land and cities back, so that whole Crusade was just a big waste of time. All

Bonifaces brothers and sisters and aunts and uncles and nephews and nieces etc etc lost their lovely palaces, they didn't have anywhere to live, they had to put all their things back in the cart. That was quite sad, actually, though Boniface was so terrible I think the Colonnas should have given them something like just a little house. So even though Boniface was so petrifying, though he was one of the most petrifying popes there ever was, he didn't get anything in the end, it was like he never was pope at all.

In the morning there was a big surprise. Chintsier already took Gabrielly away to his day care, I thought "thats good with him gone" there was just Cloudio, and then the telephone rang, it was for mum and I noticed she got a big smile, she said "but that's just wonderfull Crissy." I thought "what's this, has that nice chick found us a flat to live in?" but it wasn't that actually, Crissy said some of her cristian friends told her they might have a job for mum, it was going round showing houses to people who wanted somewhere to live. Mum said "isn't that great, and it'd be a really good way for me to find a flat for us" she said "I don't even mind if they want to convirt me, I'll go to church ten times a day if that's what it takes."

I wasn't sure, actually. I said "but what about us, if your away all day what will we do?" and Jemima was a copycat, that was good, she looked like she might cry and said "yes what about us?" That made mum go quieter again, she said "Crissy said it can be part time, I won't have to be away that long." Then Cloudio said "they could go to Gabrielley's day care, it has a school too, its very nice" but I thought "oh no, not Gabriellies" so I said "I don't want to go there" which made Cloudio go a bit cross. Mum thought a bit, she said "what about the vanhootins, they wanted you to come and learn italian with them, perhaps they won't mind if you stay a little bit later, just for now?" I thought "I suppose that wouldn't be so bad" so I said "will you take us there and collect us afterwards?" and mum said "of course, Lawrence love" she said "it probably won't even be for long, its just something to get us started." I thought "if she gets us a flat then we can get away from Gabrielley, and I can get all my things that we left at Crissys, thats good I suppose" so I said "all right then mum" and when Jemima looked like she might cry anyway I told her "it'll be good Jemima, mum will find us a flat where you can put all your dolls and animals" and it worked, she didn't cry after all, she had her toast instead.

Then Crissy rang again because she forgot something, because her friends wanted to know did mum have a car, because some of the houses were outside rome so you had to drive. That made mum worried, she said "dam I should have got someone to look at the renno, that was so stupid, I bet its been toed away by now." But Cloudio said "its probably still there, I've got a friend who fixes cars, he won't charge much, I can give him a ring if you like" and mum said "oh yes, that would be wonderfull." Then she rang Janiss pretty pig vanhootin and said could we come tomorrow, could we stay a bit later, and Janiss said "certainly" and after that she rang somebody else, she said "I just told you, can you post it straight to the bank."

Cloudios car fixer was called Loochio, he was very thin and his head sort of stuck forwards on his neck so he was a bird, I saw one like him on television once and it dived out of the air right under the water and caught a fish. He drove us in his van, we all sat in the front, I didn't have a seat belt but mum said "just this once." Soon we went out of rome and into the countryside, Loochio and mum talked and talked in italian, and I thought "I hope Cloudio's right and the car hasn't got toed away" but he was right actually, when we went into autogrill there it was in the car park. It hadn't even been robed by thieves, everything was just the same, and when I looked through the window there were some bits of old pizza beside Jemimas car seat. That was strange, because we had only got to Rome a few days ago but already it seemed like ages since we were stuck here and I got Ugo the cheese truck man to come and help.

Loochio tried the car key but the car didn't go, it didn't do anything, it didn't make a noise. Then he opened the hood, I went round to watch, and he looked at the engine, he frowned a lot so I thought "uhoh" but then suddenly he noticed something, he laughed and pulled up a wire, he showed us the end and he said "la batteriyer" so I thought "thats good, whats that?" He leaned over and screwed the wire in, then he got into the drivers seat and tried the car key and d'you know it just worked, the engine started at once. Mum laughed, she said "so it was just a wire from the battery, oh god, even I could have seen that, I feel such a fool" and I was a bit cross with Ugo hipopotomus, I thought "why didn't you notice?" but it didn't really matter, I thought "hurrah hurrah, our car works again."

We drove back, mum followed Loochio so we wouldn't get lost, and we parked in front of Cloudios house, we didn't need a ticket because it was the suburbs. Mum paid Loochio his money, she gave him four blue yuro notes but he gave one back because fixing our car was so easy, and after that when we went to a bar and had pizzas mum said "you know I'd really like to do something for Cloudio and chintsier, they've been so kind having us to stay, lets give them a nice suprise, lets cook them dinner tonight." She said she would make a curry, she likes doing them, but then when we went round the supermarket looking for ingriedients she shook her head, she said "its amazing they don't even have fresh jinger" and so eventually she got some little glass pots, she said "it won't be as nice but it'll have to do".

After that we went back to Cloudios, mum had her key, and we cooked and cooked for ages. We made chicken curry and potato curry and some other things, I helped chop the onions and Jemima broke a cup. After a bit Chintsier came back with Gabrielly and she looked at the chicken curry in its pot and said "how lovely" but her face was funny like she just ate a beetle by mistake so I thought "you are still cross because I turned Gabriellies ear like clock work, which isn't fair actually because he started it" I thought "you arent a nice squirrel any more, you are a nasty squirrel."

But Cloudio was friendly when he came back. He said we must celibrate that mum might get a job now so he had got a bottle of fizzy wine which was called proseco, the cork shot out like a bullet and hit the cieling but it didn't break anything. Cloudio said mums food was delicious, he had thirds, which was right because it was really nice. But of course Gabrielly cry baby didn't like it at all, he didn't even try it actually, he just made Chintsier cook him some spaggetties, and she didn't like it either, she just ate just a tiny bit and said "how intresting" but then she made a little face like she thought "yuck yuck" and she put down her knife and fork and pushed her plate away.

After that it was time to go to bed. I went into the bathroom and brushed my teeth four times like mum said, and I was going to get into my pijamers when I thought "I will just change Hermanns water" and that was when I notised. You see when I went over to Hermanns cage, it was in the corner just like usual, suddenley I saw something, because the cage door wasn't shut at all, it was wide open. I felt sick, I felt like I could not breath, I reached into his nest but of course he wasn't there, there was nothing, just empty straw. So I shouted out as loud as I could "Mum, mum, Hermanns gone." I knew what happened, there was only one thing it could be, so when she came in looking worried I said "the cage was just open, Gabrielley did it." Mum closed her eyes, she said "we don't know that, Lawrence love. Are you sure you didn't leave it open by mistake" but I never do that. I was thinking "oh no, where is poor Hermann, what if Gabriellies squashed him and thrown him in the garbage, what if he's thrown him out of the window so hes all alone in the road and a car will run him over?"

Now Cloudio and Chintsier came in too, they heard me shouting. Cloudio looked really worried, he said "we'll search the house, he must be somewhere here" and Chintsier said "don't worry Lawrence we'll find him" and she gave me a smile but I didn't believe her, I thought "you are still a nasty squirrel." I thought "where's that Gabrielly, he hasn't come has he" and then I had an idea, I thought "I will go and have a little talk with that cry baby right now." So I didn't follow the others, they were all going into the kichen, instead I went straight into Gabrielleys room, I just pushed open the door, I could hear the others all turning round and following, I didn't care what they did.

Gabrielly was sitting on his bed, I almost just grabed him by his neck and bashed him, I wanted to, I thought "I will caligula you" but mum was already coming in behind me now so I just said "what have you done with Hermann?" Mum gave me a look and then she asked him in italian, but I bet she changed it actually, because it took much longer and Gabrielley didn't get cross, he just shrugged his arms and said "non lowso" which means "I don't know." I thought "oh yes you do, you nasty lying horrible no animal Gabrielley" I thought "I will get you for this."

We looked all round the house, we looked in the sitting room and in the kitchen, in the bathroom and Cloudio and Chintsiers bedroom and in Gabrielleys room too, but we didn't find him, I didn't think we would, I thought "lets look in the garbage." But then there was a surprise, because suddenly Jemima came running up, she said "I just heard a funny noise, it was in our bed" and d'you know when we looked there was Hermann. He had sort of sneaked between the side and the matrass, I could just see a bit of his fur, so he was all right, he hadn't been squashed after all. I said "hurrah hurrah" and Jemima said "hurrah" too and mum looked really pleased, so did Cloudio, he said "I'm so glad" and even Gabrielley made a smile but that wasn't real of course, that was just pretending.

Cloudio took out the matrass and though Hermann tried to run away I got him, he tried to squeeze out of my hands so I thought "you really like being in this sofer bed" I said "no you don't." Afterwards I put his cage right next to my side so I could watch him when I woke up in the night and make sure he was still there. Then when we were all ready to go to bed, I put a chair up against the door handle, just like we used to in the cottage to stop dad. Mum gave me a look, she said "Lawrence love, I really don't think that's necessery" but I said "I'm not letting that Gabrielley sneek in here and get Hermann so hes lost forever" and mum didn't say anything, she just went to bed.

EMPEROR DOMITIAN WAS FAT but he had thin legs and his toes stuck out sideways a bit so they were like ducks feet, nobody liked him because he kept executing them. One day a prophet made a prophecy about him and it was really terrible, he said "you will get assasinated and it will be quite soon actually." Then he told Domitian what day it would happen, he said "it will be before six o'clock."

Domitian got really worrid, he thought "uhoh, this is awful, what can I do?" he thought "I must make a plan." First he exicuted lots of people, he executed them if they made a rude joke about him years ago, or if they carried a map of the world around them, because that was the sort of thing only emperors did, it was just in case they were going to assassinate him. After that he looked all round his palace for places where he might get assassinated, he thought "I bet its in the colonaide where I go for a walk" so he had the walls polished until they were like mirrors, so he could see if anyone came sneaking up with a dager to stab him.

Then he had a different idea, he thought "I know, I will proove that all prophets are wrong." So he went to a very famous prophet and he asked him "tell me then, how will you die?" and the prophet said "I will get eaten by dogs, actually." Domitian clapped his hands, he was so pleased, and he said "then I order you to be executed straight away by being burnt on a big fire with logs." His soldiers got lots of logs and they put the prophit on top, they lit it and Domitian thought "that's good, now everybody will see how stupid those prophits are, I will go home." But that was a mistake in fact, because after he went there was a huge wind, it was like a hurricain and all the logs on the fire got blown over, the prophets body fell down and suddenly a whole lot of dogs rushed up and ate it, so the prophet was right. When Domitian heard he said "oh no, that's bad, it didn't work after all."

Finally the day came when Domitian would get assasinated. He thought "I will just have to be really careful." First he scratched a big boil on his head and made it bleed because he hoped that would be enough to stop the prophecy, he thought "perhaps that will do." After that he walked round and round his palace, it was huge, it was so quiet he could hear his shoes go "tap tap tap." He walked along the corridors and round the garden with its pretty flowers, he carried a big dager just in case, because he didn't trust anyone, he didn't trust the cooks or the cleaners or his gardners or his best freinds or his body guards, he gave everybody suspicious looks, and when he got to the colonaide he looked behind him in the polished wall to see if anybody was sneaking up on him, but nobody was.

It seemed like that day went on for ages, Domitian thought "its like it will never stop." But finally it got later so he asked one of his servants "what time is it?" and the servant said "oh, its just after six o'clock." Domitian said "six o'clock, really?" and he was so pleased, he shouted "hurrah hurrah, I am still all right, and the prophecy said I would get killed before six, which means it was wrong after all." He thought "perhaps scratching that boil was enough" so he put down his dager and said "I know, I will go and have a lovely bath."

But actually this was a big mistake because it was all a trick, you see. Because the servant told him the wrong time, it was still only five o'clock really. Domitian went to the bathroom, he ran a nice big bath and then suddenly another servant came in. He had his arm in bandeges for days, he said it was because he broke it, but that was a trick too, because he had a dager hidden secretly in the bandages. Now he got it out and Domitian thought "oh no, this is terrible, I wish I'd brought my dager." which was right, because the servant stabed him and stabed him, Domitian could not stop him because he just had a little towel. So he was assassinated, even though he was so careful, even though he was emporer he couldn't do anything, that prophet was right after all.

The next morning mum woke us up early, she said "time to go to the vanhootins" but I didn't want to go, I said "I'm not leaving Hermann, what if Gabrielley gets him?" Mum said "don't be silly Lawrence, I'm sure it was just an accident, and anyway Gabrielly won't even be here, he'll be at his day care, remember" but I said "what if he comes home early, what if he pretends he is ill?" I said "I'll only go if you put him somewhere really high up where Gabrielly can't get him." So we put him on a high cubord in the kitchen, and mum got annoyed because she couldn't reach so she had to ask Cloudio, she said "Lawrence is worried a cat might come in" which was a lie of course. I thought Hermann might be scared of being so high but then I thought "its better than getting squashed and thrown in the garbage."

We went to the Vanhootins in our car. Mum had never driven in Rome before, she always walked or went by bus when she lived here years ago, and we got lost three times, she kept shouting "for gods sake" or "I just don't believe what he just did." But eventually we got there, Manuella opened the door, and mum had to hurry because there were some cars behind her honking, I said "be careful driving back mum, don't crash."

Our teacher was called siniora Morrow and she was nice, she was really funny, when you got it wrong she made big cross eyes and pinched your nose but it didn't really hurt, it was just a joke, she talked so fast it was like she couldn't keep still, she was a jumping puma. She taught us "commistiy" which means "how are you" and "me keyamo Lawrence" which means "I'm called Lawrence." Little Leonora mouse was better at italian than big Tina bossy rabbit, that was a surprise and it made Tina cross. Another surprise happened when we were having lunch, which was Manueller's lovely sandwiches, because Tina and Leonora kept saying "mum, can we go to the dvd shop later" or "can we go out and have pizza" but Janiss pretty pig didn't answer them because she was always too busy, she was reading a magazeen or talking on the telephone, she said "not now girls" so I thought "that's strange" because mum always answers us straight away, even if she just says "don't be silly."

Another strange thing was that Tina and Leonora hardly had

any toys, they just had a few dolls and games and things which were quite boring, we had tons more at the cottage, actually we had brought more to Rome in our car. So I felt a bit sorry for those little Vanhootins, even bossy rabbit, and I told them "when we get a flat you can come over and play with our toys, we've got lots."

When mum came to collect us she was cheerful, she said she met Crissies cristian friends and they said yes, you can have this job and they didn't ask her to go to church ten times a day after all, that was good, mum said she went to the British embassy too and got her new passport. When we walked back to where she parked the car she said "the only bad news is that I don't think they've got a flat for us" she said "they had a look in their books but everything was so expensive, I couldn't believe it. They said our best chance was asking everyone we know in case someone has something cheaper." Jemima was silly, she tried to help, she said "lets ask everyone right now mummy, lets ask him" and she pointed at a man, he looked at us like he was very surprised, he was cleaning the road with a brush. I thought "if only we knew someone like pope Bonniface, he would get us a nice place" I said "you must know some other Romans mum" and she said "I suppose there are my old students, I'm sure they've all moved ten times since then but I could try and look them up, I remember one was a countess." I didn't know countess, but mum said it was a bit like being the queen but smaller, so I said "oh yes, I bet she has thousands of flats" but mum said "there are lots of countesses in Rome, Lawrence, and some don't have any flats at all" she said "but we can always try."

Another thing she said was that we must babysit Gabrielley tonight, which was because Cloudio and Chintsier were both going out, Cloudio had a meeting and Chintsier had to eat supper in a restaurant for her work. I thought "that's good actually, because I'll be able to watch that sneaky no animal and make sure he doesn't do anything horrible to Hermann."

Then when we got near Cloudio's house and mum parked the car a funny thing happened, I remember it. Mum walked down the road a little bit and then she said "look at that car parked over there, its just the same color as your fathers" it was yellow. I said "his is a bit paler" but mum said "no, its just the same, I'm sure of it" so I said "but his is different, its bigger" and mum said "oh yes" but she still went up and had a really good look in the windshield.

After that we went back to Cloudio's house. I got a bit worried, I thought "what if Gabrielly went home early, what if he pretended he was ill, what if he got a ladder" but fortunatley he hadn't, Hermann was still on the cuboard. Mum got him down, she climbed on the table, and I gave him new water and seeds, and actually the babysitting was really easy. Gabrielly didn't do anything awful, I gave him some Calligula looks when mum wasn't watching and I think that helped, because he hardly said anything and he ate the spagetties mum made. When I was brushing my teeth Cloudio bear came home because his meeting finished early, and he put Gabrielly to bed, so mum didn't have to do that, which was good too.

Then suddenly I woke up, it was because there was a noise, and though I was asleep when the noise happened I could still remember it, that was funny, it was like it was on a Cd in my head and I could play it again if I wanted. It was a scrapeing noise, I thought "I bet that's a chair." I looked around and though it was dark I could see because there was a bit of light beside the curtains. Hermann was there in his cage, he was awake, he usually is in the night, he is nocturnel, and he was sticking his nose through the bars and looking at a wall, I thought "hes all right, that's good." Mum wasn't there, she often goes away again once we are sleeping, so I thought "she probably made that scraping noise" so that was all right too.

But then I had another thought, I thought "what if it wasn't mum at all, what if its Gabrielly?" Then I thought "what could he do when everybodies sleeping?" and I thought "well, he might go in the kitchen where my box is and he might start wrecking all my tintins" I thought "he might put my hotwheels in the garbage." After that I thought "no, he's probably not doing that, he's probably just asleep" but then I thought "but he might be" and d'you know that thought just wouldn't go away, it wouldn't budge, it kept coming back until it made me go all awake, it made me get really cross. So I thought "he'd better dam well not be doing that, that little sneaky, nasty no animal." Now I thought "perhaps I'd better just go and see" and I got up from the sofa bed, but then I stopped, because I thought "what if it's a trick, what if I go out and then he sneaks in behind me and does something terrible to Hermann?" But then I thought "no he can't, not if I'm really quick."

So I went out of the sitting room, I walked across to the kitchen, and the door was open just a tiny slit so I looked in. And it wasn't Gabrielley at all, actually, it was Cloudio and mum instead, they were sitting at the kitchen table and they had glasses of wine so I thought "thats all right then, I'll go back now before Gabrielly sneaks in behind me." But then I notised something, because Cloudio had his hand on mums back, so I thought "that's strange." I heard mum through the door, she said "don't be silly, bear, really we can't" and I thought "thats strange too, how does she know Cloudios a bear?" Then Cloudio said "her dinner won't finish till eleven and its a long way." Mum said "really bear, no" and then Cloudio made a kind of little moan like he was going to cry and he did a really funny thing, because suddenley he put his head down, it was like he was divving into a swimming pool but he put it down between mums arms, and I felt funny like I couldn't breath, it was like when I noticed that Hermanns door was wide open.

Cloudio said something, it was a bit hard to hear because he said it into mum's boddy but I heard it any way, he said "I don't care about Chintsier all I care about is you Hannah" and I thought "hes definitely going to cry now" I thought "I don't like you any more" I thought "I wish we never came here to these Cloudios because they are all awful, Chintsier nasty squirrel and Gabrielly sneaky no animal and Cloudio horrible bear, I wish we'd stayed with those nuns." Now Cloudio popped his head up again, he said "I just feel so lost." Mum said "no bear no" like she wanted him to go away, so I thought "that's right" I thought "make him go away mum, just come back to bed right now" but then something happened, that was a real surprise. Because suddenly mum reached forward with her head and she gave Cloudio a big kiss, it went on for ages and she put her fingers round his ears.

That was when I sort of went into the room. It was strange, I just found I was going in, it was like I hadn't decided at all, it was like my feet just went by themselves. I thought "uhoh" I thought "what will I do now?" then I thought "oh yes I will get a tintin." So I walked past, I didn't look, it was like I hadn't noticed they were there. I heard a chair scrapeing noise, it was just like the one I heard when I was asleep, and suddenly mum shouted out "what are you doing here, why aren't you in bed" and she said it loud like she was really cross with me.

I didn't say anything, I didn't answer, I just kept quiet and went very carefully across the room to my box and got my Tintin, it was "the crab with the golden claws" It was funny, I felt like nothing was happening, I felt like I wasn't there at all, it was like I was in space or something, but then suddenly everything just changed completly, suddenly I got really really angry, I thought "why is mum shouting at me, thats not fair, I haven't done any-thing wrong, I'm just getting my Tintin, how dare she" and I re-ally hated her for shouting at me. So I threw the crab with golden claws right across the room, I didn't even look where it went, I think it landed on the micro waive.

I ran right out of the kitchen and I slammed the door behind me as hard as I could, I didn't care if someone was behind me and they got their hand caught but nobody did. I ran straight into the sitting room, I slammed that door too, so Jemima woke up, she said "whats happening" but I didn't say anything, I could hear Gabrielley shouting, he woke up as well, and I got into bed. Mum came in, she came over to me and she said "Lawrence love I'm so so sorry" but I didn't care, I said "you shouted at me and that wasn't fair, I'm not talking to you" but she kept on talking anyway, she said "please lawrence listen, I didn't mean to shout at you, I'm so sorry, this is all a big mistake, Lawrence love, please, please." I could tell she was getting upset but dyou know I just didn't care, actually I was pleased, I thought "you go and be upset mum, you squeaze your hair and scrach your arm and say dam dam, you go sad, I don't mind." I didn't take any notice of her, I thought "I will just talk to Herman now" I said "I wish mum would just shut up and go away forever, don't you?"

CHAPTER FOUR

A long time ago when we just moved to the cottege mum said "let's have a treat today Lawrence love, let's go to Wipsinaide zoo." It was sunday, there wasn't anything to do, actually, but I felt cross, I remember it, I thought "I want to go back to Scotland, I want to see my cousins and play on Robbies computer" and I said "I don't want to go to Wipsinaide zoo I want to stay here."

So we just stayed at home, I watched telly and it was quite boring in fact. I sat in the kitchen playing with my cars and it was very quiet, I could hear the fridge going wirr wirr. After that we went to London zoo once and dad took me to Edinburuh zoo when I went to see him for his weekends but I never did go to Wipsnaide. Its strange, I think about that day sometimes. I wonder what animals there were that we never saw, and what food we didn't eat for lunch, I bet there was a cafeteria, there were ice creams, and it makes me feel funny. I think oh I wish I'd just said "yes mum lets go to Wipsnaide Zoo" but of course its too late, that day is gone away now.

I wasn't speaking to anybody in the morning at Cloudios, I only talked to Hermann, I told him "we are moving to Guses now, thats good because it will be much nicer there, you will be safe from Gabrielley." I just ate my toast, Cloudio made it but he didn't look at me, he looked at the table or the walls, so I gave him my Caligula glaire, I think he knew but he didn't look back, it was like he was scared. I thought "I don't like you Cloudio" and then I read my Calamitous Cesaers.

Emporer Nero's mother was called Agrippina and she was always shouting at Nero and ordering him around so he got really cross, he thought "how dare she say that to me." He thought "how can I stop her from shouting at me?" He was so annoyed he took away all her soldiers, he made her move out of his palace, and then he got his freinds to ride past her house on their horses and say really rude insults at her, he thought "that will stop her" but he was wrong. None of it worked, actually she shouted at him more than before, she was terrible. So he thought "all right, I will just get her killed then, I will get her assasinated, that will stop her."

First he tried to poisson her but she was too clever and she always drank the antidoate first so the poison didn't work. Then he got someone to break her bedroom ceiling really carefully so it would suddenly fall on her when she was sleeping, but she found out about this plan too, and she went to sleep in another room, so that didn't work either.

Then one day Nero had a new idea, he thought "I know I will

make a special collapsible boat." He got his servants to make the boat, it took ages and then he invited his mother round for supper at his palace by the seaside, he said "lets not have any more of these stupid arguments mum, lets be friends again." Agrippinna said "all right Nero, lets" and she came to dinner, it was very nice, it was really delicous and when they finished she said "thank you for a lovely time" and he said "not at all" so it was like they really were freinds again now.

But then they went down to the sea, it was almost dark now, and Agripina notised that her boat had sunk. Nero said "oh dear, look at your boat, it must have had an accident" which was a lie of course, because he made his servants crash it. He said "don't worry mum, you can use mine." Agrippina said "oh thank you Nero" she never guessed, and so she sailed off in the special collapsible boat. There wasn't a storm, the sea was calm, it was a lovley night, but then suddenly the boat began to collapse, pieces broke off and the masts dropped out until everything fell apart completly so there was nothing left, just little bits of wood. But Agripinna was a very good swimmer, so she and her servant swam all the way to the seashore, though it was a long way away, they were saved.

Agripina still didn't guess what happened, she thought "oh dear, that wasn't a good boat" so she sent her servant to tell Nero what happened. Nero sat on his emporers chair listening to her servant tell him that they were saved and he thought "oh no this is bad, my plan didn't work after all" but he didn't say anything, he pretended he was pleased, he smiled and said "poor mum, thank goodness shes all right." But then he got someone to sneek up behind the servant and suddenly they dropped a dager on the floor beside him, it made a loud clang and Nero shouted "oh look there, its a dager, he was trying to assasasinate me, mum must have sent him." So the servant and Aggripina were both arrested, they were executed, and he finally got her killed, he thought "hurrah."

After that Nero was worried everybody would hate him for executing his mother, he thought "I don't want to go back to Rome, because they will all shout really rude insults" but he was wrong. When he went back all the Romans were waiting along the road in their Sunday best, it was like Nero had just won a big war, they all cheered and shouted "well done Nero, thank goodness you weren't assasiniated" but it wasn't real of course, they really thought "how dreadful, he killed his own mummy" it was just so they wouldn't get executed. So Nero thought "hurrah, I'm all right after all."

But then a strange thing happened. Suddenly Nero knew his mother was watching him. It was her goast actually, he couldn't see her but he knew she was there, he could feel it, she followed him everywhere and now she shouted at him even more crossly than before because he executed her. Nero thought "this is terrible" he thought "I wonder how I can make her go away?" He got special wizerds from Persher to do spells to make her appear, so he could say "I'm really sorry mum for executing you, now please just leave me alone" but the spells didn't work, they never suceeded, and she never did appear. So he never got rid of her actually, her goast followed him for years and years, it never left him alone until he was dead too.

It wasn't just me who wasn't speaking in the morning, because hardly anybody was. Chintsier wasn't speaking, she just stood by the sink with cross arms and slit eyes, so I thought "she really really hates us now." Cloudio wasn't speaking either, his eyes were funny like he swiched them off, it was like he was hiding behind them so he wouldn't cry, I thought "go on Cloudio cry, cry a lot." And Gabrielly wasn't speaking, but that wasn't because he was cross, actually he was really cheerful now we were going away. As soon as mum finished packing our bags he got lots of his toys and put them all in the sitting room instead of us, then he switched on the telly really loud and he sat there watching it. In fact the only one who was speaking that morning was Jemima and she wouldn't stop, she kept saying "I want some more choclate serial" or "why are we going away again?" or "I don't want to go to Guses, I want to go back to Crissies, I want all my animals and my dolls." Mum answered in a funny voice, it was sort of squeeking, and her smile was too big like it might just go "pop" she said "lamikin we can't crowd out poor Cloudio and Chintsier any longer."

I didn't help pack the car, I let Cloudio and mum carry everything, I thought "you do it." I just took Hermann, I put his cage on the seat beside me and I told him "we don't ever have to come back here again, Hermann, thats good isn't it" and I don't know if Cloudio heard, he was quite near, he might have. Then we drove off and I didn't wave goodbye.

Mum got lost twice, she almost hit a red car and she said "it says we're not supposed to go down here, oh god" then finally we got to Guses. A car behind us couldn't go past because the road was too narrow and it started honking, so Mum ran out really fast and rang the doorbell. Then lots of people came out, one was Gus, and they got all our things. Gus took Hermanns cage, I said "bye bye Hermann, don't worry I'll come back soon" and though they all smiled and waved at me I didn't smile and wave back, I just didn't feel like it. I thought "I don't like any of you new Gus dog people, I'm not going to think what animals you have, that means you don't have any."

There were two cars honking now and mum had one leg in the car and one leg out, she said "where can I park?" Gus lifted his hands in the air like this was the funniest thing, he said "Hannah, your in the middle of rome, you'll be lucky if you find anything. The free parking spaces have white lines." So we drove round and round looking for white lines but there were hardly any, they were all blue or yellow, and they all had cars in them anyway. We drove round for hours, Jemima fell asleep, till finally we were going up a hill, the road went round and round like a big snake, and I could see Rome out of the window with all its doames and rooves, then suddenly mum braked really hard so we swerved a bit, the car made a noise like in a film, and we went right in a parking place with white lines, mum said "oh thank god."

I watched mum as she woke up Jemima and got her out of her seat, she was all slow and floppy from being asleep so mum had to carry her. Then Mum opened my door, she said "come on Lawrence" and it was funny, I didn't feel cross until then, I just sat in the car as we drove round and round, I watched all the cars and the motorcycles and buildings out of the window, I wasn't thinking anything at all, I was just thinking "that's a funny looking car" or "theres a really big doame" but now when mum opened my door suddenly I got really really cross, I thought "you shouted at me in Cloudios kitchen, you put your fingers on his ears." So I didn't move, I just sat there and looked out of the windshield, there was a bird fighting another bird so it could get some crums. Mum gave me a look, she said "Lawrence, please" and her voice started getting annoyed, so I thought "don't you get cross with me, don't you start shouting again" and I said "I want to go back to england, I don't like Rome, its horreble."

Mum gave me a funny look, it was like she was cross and she was scared, she didn't know which, and she said "for goodness sake Lawrence, you know we can't do that." Then I looked at Jemima, she was rubbing her eyes, and I said "I want to go home to the cottage so I can play with all my toys there, and Jemima can play with all her other dolls and her marbles game and her spirograff." Those were some of her favorite things that she left behind actually, so she sort of woke up more and she said "I want to go home too."

Now Mum got really cross, she said "I haven't time for this" she put Jemima down on the ground and she reached into the car to get me. But I was ready, I thought "no you don't" and when her arm went past to undo my seat belt I got it with my hands and then I bit it really hard with my teeth. That was a big surprise for mum, she shreeked and she pulled her arm out so fast, and Jemima laughed, she thought "this is a funny game" but then she saw our faces and she started crying instead. Mum said "Lawrence" and she stood there staring at me. I thought "go on mum, cry" but she didn't, so I thought "she isn't going sad anymore" I thought "that's a shame, I want her to get sad." I thought "if she isn't going to cry then she'll go really cross" but she didn't do that either. She looked at me like she was just really tired and she said "what is it you want from me Lawrence?"

I thought for a bit, I thought "what can I have?" and I said "I want a treat, a really good treat." Mum frowned like I was horrible and she said "all right all right, you can have your dam treat." I thought "I must check" so I said "anything I want, anything at all?" and mums eyes went really big because she was annoyed, she said "yes, anything you want."

So we had pizzas, and then we got a bus that went almost to Piazza Nevoner where the toy shops were. Because I could have anything I wanted, which never happened usually, I thought "I must be really careful, I mustn't get it wrong" so I took a long time. I went to both the toy shops three times, I looked at all the shelves to make sure I didn't miss anything, and then finally I chose my treat, it was a radio controlled car, it was really big and its head lights lit up. I said "I want that, and I want its batteries too." Mum got cross, she closed her eyes and she said "Lawrence, for goodness sake, that's more than a hundred yuros, why not have this one, it's a third of the price and its almost the same" but I shook my head, I thought "your not going to cheete me out of my treat" and I said "no I want this one, you said I could have anything I want, you promised, remember."

Mum told the shop lady and she got it down, and Jemima got a doll that was floppy like clothes because Jemima always has to have something too, but when we went to pay mum's card didn't work. Mum said "oh god" she said "look Lawrence, I bet it will work if we get that other car" but I thought "no you don't" and I said "what about your blue card because that worked when we went to that restaurant." So we went to a cashpoint machine, it was quite far, it was by the panthion, mum got out the money, she said "that'll be the last of it" and I said "come on mum, hurry up."

We got the car and we put in the batteries, we got the man in the shop to do it because you needed a screw driver, and then I made it go in the Piazza Nevona. The lights didn't light up after all, that was just in the picture on the box, that was annoying. Mum and Jemima sat on a stone bench and watched, mum said "are you happy now" which meant she was cross, but I didn't say anything. It was a bit borring once I got used to the controls, I made it go round and round a fountain until the batteries began to run out so it went more and more slowly, it sort of creped. I thought "I don't much like this treat actually" I thought "maybe I will let us stay in Rome, maybe I won't."

WHEN WE WENT BACK TO GUSES they were all in the sitting room which was the kitchen too, they were drinking wine, and I thought "this is old and dirty" I thought "I don't like it here." They all said "welcome to our house" and mum said "this is so kind of you" and then she said "come on Lawrence, say hello, don't be unfreindly" but I didn't say hello, I just didn't feel like it, so mum said "he's a bit tired today" which just was a lie of course. But then I changed my mind. I thought "even if its old and dirty here its still better than being at Cloudios." So I looked at all the people, there were five of them, and I thought "and you are not Cloudio and Chintsier and Gabrielly" I thought "all right then, I suppose I will give you your animals after all."

Gus didn't need one of course, he was already a dog, he asked mum "so how was Cloudios" and mum said "it was lovely, but I just didn't want to croud them out in that little flat" which was another lie, I thought "what a lot of lies your saying today mum." Gus said he was writing a play for doing in a theater, Mum said "but you were doing that last time" and Gus said "this is completely different, this is much angrier" so I thought "that's silly, how can a play get angry?"

Next to Gus there was Marther who had funny eyes, she looked right at you with a special smile, it was like she was saying "I am Martha and I am looking at you" so she was Marther the special monkey, I thought "do I like you marther?" I thought "I'm not sure." She asked me what I liked best at school and when I said "stories" she was pleased, she said I would like this house because everybody here was an artist, they were all writing or singing or something. I said "but an artist doesn't sing, an artist does paintings" but Marther said "no, Lawrence, a singer can be an artist too, like Oska here" and she pointed at Oska, who was sitting in the corner with his giutar, she said "Osker is our song writer" and Oska laughed, he said "no he is your busker" which I knew, because mum told me once, it is somebody who sings outside restaraunts so people give him money. Marther said "Oska will be the next Bob Dillin you just wait" but I didn't know Bob

Dillin, I wanted to ask mum but I didn't because I was still cross with her.

Oska was very thin with black hair and he only played his guitar a bit sometimes, so it was like he was talking with it actually, it said "oh yes" or "no I don't think so" he was a smiley guitar ferrit. Marther said "your all staying in Oskas' room actually, he's sleeping down here on the sofa, we so wanted to help you" and mum said "that's so kind, Oska, I really don't know how to thank you" and he didn't say anything, he just smiled and made his guitar go "pling pling pling" like it was saying "that's ok" which was funny.

So I thought "actually you new people are quite nice after all I suppose, even greedy Gus and Marther special monkey" I thought "I'm glad I'm giving you your animals." My favorite was Hilary, she was chopping vegtables and putting them in pots, she had brown hair that was round like a ball and she was fat, whenever she looked at me she gave me a nice smile, so she was a nice cow. Martha said Hillary was brilliant at cooking, one day she would have lots of restaraunts all over the world, and Hilery made a funny smile, she said "I don't know about that."

The last one was really easy to get an animal for. He was called Freddy and he had a white beard which was so big it was bigger than his head, and it was frizzy like stuff that comes out of cushions if theres a hole, so he was Freddy the Father Chrismas Bear. Freddy talked like Bill Vanhootin, Marther said he was from Canada, which is near America, she said "Freddies our brilliant poet, he had his poems published in a book, and now hes helping me write poems too, poor fool" and Freddy said "Marther's really

115

good." Then Marther gave him her special smile and she said "Freddy, maybe you should show Hannah Lawrence and Jemima round the house."

So we saw all the rooms. Hilary nice cow had a blue bottle on the table with a flower in it, Freddy said "Hilleries our angel, she looks after us all." There was a computer room, mum had a computer like that ages ago when I was small, so I thought "thats really old" but Freddy liked it, he said "feel free to use it any time, just put a yuro in the trust box" and mum said "that's kind." Guses room was almost empty, there were just some books and a bed that was flat on the floor like a carpit. Next door was Martha special monkeys room but it was locked, Jemima tried the handle, Freddy said "Marthers the boss, this is her house" and mum said "just leave it alone, Jemima." Our room was upstairs and it had a bed like a carpet like Guses, Hermann and all our bags were there. So I went to say hello to Hermann, I said "I told you I'd come back" and then I looked out of the window at the road, two ladies were looking at a shop, and I thought "its not very nice but its much better than horrible Cloudios house" I thought "all right I will let us stay here."

Freddy chrismas bear said "I'm next door, if you ever need anything just shout." So we went to see his room which had funny pens, they were very long and thin and mum said they weren't pens actually, they were quils. But the really intresting thing was the pieces of paper which were stuck all over the walls, there were hundreds, so you could hardly see the walls at all. Freddy said "those are my poems, I like to have them up so I can look at them and write them better." Then Jemima blew like she was blowing out a candel and some of them moved, it was like they wanted to go off flying, so of course she blew at them again and I thought "uhoh, watch out, poemes" but they were saved, because then Hilary nice cow shouted up the stairs, she said "dinners ready."

Usually mum says I must eat some vegetables but this time she forgot so I just ate pasta with cheese. The reason she forgot was because she was talking and talking with Gus, he was telling her about how his play was so angry and she was telling him how lovely it was being in Rome again, it was just so wonderfull. At first I didn't mind but then I got annoyed, I thought "I'm watching you mum" I thought "you'd better not be like you were in Cloudios kitchen" I thought "you'd better not put your fingers on Guses ears."

Then something happened, because the telephone rang, Hillery got it, she said "it's for you Hannah" and she gave mum a funny look, she made her eyebrows go up and she said "its someone called Beppo." I thought "oh yes, Beppo who I don't know and who Franseen and Crissy chick and me don't like at all." Mum started talking and talking on the telephone, she said "how amazing, how clever of you to track us down." Now Gus looked cross, so I thought "that's good, ha ha Gus" but only for a bit, because mum went on and on, she wouldn't stop and she was smiling and smiling so I thought "you really like this Beppo." Everyone was quiet, I thought "they are all listening" mostly it was in Italian but some bits were in english, she said "really, oh god that would be so good, actually we are getting a bit desperate." Finally she stopped, she said "till tomorrow then" and Gus said "Beppo, wasn't he the one who used to drive round in that open top" which I didn't know, mum said it was a car without a roof. Mum said "that's right, and he said he might have a flat for us, isn't that wonderful" but I thought "I don't know about that" I thought "I don't like your flat Beppo."

After that it got worse, because mum started talking and talking to Gus all over again. I thought "this is really enough now, its like it just goes on forever" I thought "there are so many of them, these Guses and Cloudios and Beppos, I cant stop them all." Then I noticed an intresting thing, because Marther looked cross too. She said "can you get us some more wine Gus" so I thought "I know, you are trying to interupt them" I thought "go on, Marther" but it didn't work, Gus got the wine but then he just started talking to mum all over again. I tried too, I said "mum, I want a tintin, the red sea sharks, can you go up stairs and get it out of the bag" but that didn't work either, she said "not now Lawrence, can't you see I'm still having my dinner." I thought "how long are you going to be, are you going to be ages?" so I looked at her plate, and d'you know it was like she told a big lie, because there was just a tiny bit left, it was sitting on her fork, it would all go in one bite easily. I thought "you are being on slow on purpose" I thought "you are keeping that bit so you don't have to get my tintin, its so you can say you are still eating so you can go on talking and talking with Gus, its so you can do his ears" and suddenly something happened. I felt so cross, I could feel it in my stomack and arms, it was in my teeth, it was like it might lift me right up, and I thought "I wonder what will happen now" I thought "I wonder what I will do?"

I looked at Jemima, her eyes were going funny like she would go to sleep in her chair, and I thought "I think I will wake you up" so I said "Jemima, d'you want to come and play with Hermann?" which worked of course, her eyes went wide open straight away. When I got up from the table mum gave us a little smile so I thought "oh yes, your pleased we're going away." We went upstairs to our room, I got Hermann out, I let her hold him just for a bit, I let her change his water and put more food in his bowl, and when we finished I said "I'm going into Freddies room now to look at his poems and his funny pens but you can't come, all right Jemima, because you will break them. You have to go back downstairs right now." I thought "you'd better not follow me, Jemima, or it will be your fault." But d'you know that's just what she did, she ran straight after me, that was silly, so I warned her, I said "Jemima, I just told you that you couldn't come in."

It was funny standing in Freddies room without mum or Freddy, it was all quiet. I said to Jemima "you mustn't touch any of Freddies funny pens, all right?" and d'you know what she did, she made her bad face and then she ran over and grabed one though I just said she mustn't, that was stupid. I could see her hand was all inky now, so I said "Jemima, I just told you you mustn't do that, now give that to me right now or I will hit you on the head with a pillow." But she didn't lisen at all, she just did her squeaking laugh and ran into the corner with her back to me so I couldn't get the pen off her. I thought "I warned you Jemima" so I got a pillow from Freddies bed and I went up and hit her on the head, but she just gigelled, and I noticed all of Freddies poemes on the walls were going "flap flap" because the pillow made a little breeze, I thought "look at those."

After that I hit Jemima with the pillow again, which was because she wasn't listening, and I said "don't hit me with a pillow, Jemima, you really mustn't all right" and d'you know that's just what she did, she just dropped her quil and then ran over to Freddies bed and got one. I thought "uhoh you've made it all inky with your hand Jemima, now that will be staned forever." I thought "uhoh, what bad thing will she do next?" I thought "I must stop her" so I said "whatever you do you mustn't do this" and I hit the wall a bit with my pillow. It was just to make her see what she mustn't do, but some of the poemes fell down, it was an accident, I thought "that silly Chrismas Bear didn't stick them on properly, he should have used more selotape."

Now Jemima did something really bad, she hit another wall and it wasn't an accident at all, it was on purpose, so suddenly lots of poems came off. I said "look what you've done" I thought "I will stop her now" and I tried to get her pillow off her by hitting it with my pillow, I think I hit a few poemes by mistake, but it didn't work anyway, because she was holding her pillow too tight. I thought "you are so bad, Jemima" because now there were poems everywhere, they were flying in the air and they were all over the floor, it was like it was raining poems, but it was Jemima who jumped up and down on them, I didn't do that, I only trod on a few because I was trying to stop her, they were all slippy and scrunchey under my feet.

I thought "I know, I will stop her in a different way" so I ran out of Freddys room. I had to take my pillow because she took hers but I didn't want to fight any more, I said "stop it Jemima" but she wouldn't, she followed me right into Guses room, so it was her fault his books got knocked off the shelf. I said "Jemima no" and I ran down the stairs, I just threw away my pillow, I said "don't hit me Jemima" but she didn't listen. She was squeeking like she thought "I can really get him now" she was gigelling like she would go "pop" and when we ran into the dining room she hit me on my arm but then she saw them all staring at us and her mouth went open like a fish.

Mum looked like a big bee just stung her, she stopped talking to Gus dog, and d'you know what she said, that wasn't fair, she said "Lawrence what are you doing." I thought "how dare you mum" I said "it wasn't me, it was Jemima" I said "look I haven't even got a pillow." But Jemima is a big cheet, she is a liar, her lips wobbled and she started crying, so I thought "you are trying to win just by crying" I thought "no you don't" and I said "she was the one who knocked down Freddies poemes." Now Freddy got stung by a bee, he jumped up from his chair and mum said "Lawrence what have you done" which was stupid, because didn't I just tell her it was Jemima? Everything went quiet, Freddy ran upstairs and then there was a kind of moan, he found his poems, so I thought "now you will know you must use more selotape."

Marther gave mum a look, it was like she was a bit pleased actually, that was funny, and she said "Hannah if you want to stay in our house then you must keep your children under controll" and mum looked like she would go double triple "pop" she would just burst, she said "Lawrence and Jemima, you will both say your sorry right now" and d'you know I knew just what to say, it just came into my head, I said it before Jemima could say anything,

I thought "this is the right thing" I said "I don't like you mum, I really hate you" and then I ran up to the bath room before she could get me and I locked the door.

Mum came up lots of times, she banged on the door with her hand "thump thump thump" and she shouted that I must let her in right this moment, Lawrence, I must say I'm sorry and help clear up this dam mess, but I didn't say anything, I just sat on the floor next to the key hole so I could hear. First they went into Guses room and mum said "I'm so sorry about all this Marther, really I am, he's never like this usually" but Marther was still cross, she said "we really can't have this sort of behavior, we are artists here, we need our peace and quiet." Jemima tried to clean up a bit, I could hear her saying "where does this go?" so I thought "you won't be much use." Then I heard Gus but he wasn't angry actually, he was joking, he said "my rooms pre-recked, I can't see much difference" so I thought "why aren't you cross now, go on, be cross, I don't like you Gus."

After that they all went up to Freddies room, they were quieter because it was upstairs but I could still hear them, mum did a kind of shreek, she said "oh god, I can't believe this." I couldn't hear what Freddy said but his voice wasn't cross actually, it sounded like he was telling mum "don't get too angry with him" so I thought "thank you Chrismas bear."

Then a strange thing happened. It was like my crossness started going away. It was like when you have a bath and you let all the water go down the plug hole but you don't get out, you are still sitting there and suddenly you just feel cold. I thought "someone will want to go to the loo soon but I don't want to see any of them, I don't want to open the door, so I will get stuck in here" I thought "uhoh, what will I do?" But they were still talking upstairs, they weren't coming down yet, so then I thought "I will just go right now." I opened the door and I ran upstairs carefully, I didn't make any noise. I could see Guses foot and the bottom of his leg sticking out of Freddies door but it didn't move, he didn't look round, so I just ran into our room, I shut the door really quietly, I got into my pijamers and I got into the bed, then I shut my eyes so it was like I had been asleep for hours.

Eventually the door opened, I heard Jemima say "look mum theres Lawrence" and I thought "uhoh, mum will shout at me now, this will be bad" but she didn't, she didn't say anything, I thought "that's funny." I didn't move at all, I could hear mum getting Jemima in her pijamas, she said "there you are lamikin" I felt the bed go down when they got in, and then mum switched the light off. Jemima went to sleep really quick like she always does, but then just when I thought "hurrah hurrah, I am all right after all" mum said in a wisper "Lawrence, I know your awake" so I thought "oh no, here it comes." I thought "her voice will be like a stick" but it wasn't at all, that was strange. It wasn't cross or sad or nice or anything, it was just nothing, it was like she was saying "oh yes we need to get some more milk" or "what dyou want for your breakfast?" But it was funny, because it was even worse because she wasnt cross after all, I thought "I wish you were just shouting actually" I thought "you really hate me now."

Mum said "I'm sorry about what happened at Cloudios Lawrence" but she didn't sound sorry, she sounded like I was her enimy now. I thought "now I will be cross again, its my turn" but it didn't work, I just thought "this is dreadfull, everybody hates me, I bet even Jemima hates me except she is asleep." Mum was quiet for a long time so I thought "has she gone to sleep too?" but then she said "theres something you should know, Lawrence. When I lived here years ago Cloudio and me were very close, I hadn't met your father then and he hadn't met Chintsier. In fact he wanted us to get married, but I didn't want to marry him, and that made him very sad." I thought "I'm glad" I thought "you leave my mum alone, Cloudio from ages ago before I was born, you just go away and be sad." Mum said "but I never thought he still liked me like that now. When you saw us I was just trying to tell him no, Cloudio, this is imposible." I thought "no you werent, mum that's a big lie" and it was like I wanted to cry, I said "but you put your fingers on his ears, I saw it." But mum just went on in her nothing voice, she said "I was just trying to stop him from getting more upsit."

I thought "its good if he gets upset" and I said "what about Gus, does he want to get married too?" I thought "mum will just say poor Gus is sad as well" but she didn't at all, suddenly she sounded really cross, she said "for goodness sake, is that what all this is about then Lawrence" she said "Gus isn't intrested in getting married to anyone." I said "but he was talking and talking to you" and mum said "this is so stupid. Gus just likes talking, but he's only intrested in himself. In fact if Gus married anyone he'd marry himself."

I didn't want to laugh, I wanted to be really serious, but it was so hard, because it was just so funny thinking Gus will get married to himself, he will be mr and mrs Gus dog. I tried to sort of put my laughing in a box, but then it all just came out in a big kind of snort and after that I couldn't stop. That was bad, because mum didn't laugh at all, she was just quiet like she was thinking "you are so stupid" she said "stop it Lawrence, you'll wake Jemima" so I thought "you really really hate me now." I thought "why did I think Gus dog was horrible, that was silly" and suddenly I just wanted to hide under the bed, though this was impossible of course because it was just a matrass on the floor, nobody could go under it, not even a beetle. I thought "I wish I hadn't done that pillow fight. I wish I hadn't done Guses books and Freddies quils and poems."

Then mum started again in her serious voice. She said "Lawrence this is a very difficult time for us" she said "we don't have anywhere to live, we need peoples help, cant you see that?" so I said "yes mum." She said "I want you to promise you'll behave really well to everybody from now on, will you do that?" After that she stopped, she was waiting. I didn't really want to promise actually, I don't know why, but I knew I had to. I thought "mum hates me now, and if I don't promise then I bet she will really really hate me, she will probably hate me forever" so I just did it, I made myself. I said "I promise mum" and she gave a hug, it wasn't a really big one but I didn't care, I wanted it.

THE SUN IS MADE OF GAS, it is soft, it is like a big hot jelly. The middle of the sun is like a bomb, it is always blowing up and this makes waves go out, they make the edges vibrate in and out every few minutes so its almost like the sun is breatheing.

Scientists looked at it a lot, they had to use special telescopes because it is so bright, you must never look at it just with your eyes or they will get burnt out, you will go blind. Scientists noticed the sun is always changing, sometimes its just normal, it is quiet, but then slowly it gets busier, its like it gets angry, it takes years and years. First it gets sun spots, they are colder than the rest but they are still really hot of course, they are boilling, and they are really huge, they are as big as a planet. Then when the sun gets really angry it spits out flares, they are made of electric gas which is called plasma, and they shoot out like huge arms, they explode like bombs.

One day the Sientists looked up and saw that a flare was coming right at earth, and though we are millions of miles away, it was coming really fast, they thought "uhoh its going to hit us" but it was all right, everybody was safe because it was stopped by something called the magnetic field, so it didn't blow us up after all, actually nobody even notised.

But then scientists thought "those flares could be really dangerous." Because they might hit satelites that are up in space, because they are not protected by the magnetic field at all, they will get broken, and then suddenly peoples sellphones and televisions won't work any more, it will be a disaster. Scientists got so worried that one day they built a special satellite, it is called soho and it is far away in space, it watches the sun all the time really carefully and says if its making a terrible flair that will come right for earth. Then the scientists will say "switch off all the satelites right now." But I think they must be really quick or it will be too late, the satelites will get broken after all. Then nobodies television will work so they will miss their favorite programs, and their sell phones won't work either, which will be really bad, because they won't get any warnings.

The next morning I thought "I don't want to meet any of those animals, Freddy chrismas bear or Gus dog or Marther, I just don't." Mum said "up you get you two, your going to the van-hootins, I've got to get to work" but when we went out of our room I notised all their doors were closed so I thought "oh thank goodness they're still sleeping." I said "lets be really quiet Jemima, its a new game."

Mum took us to the Vanhootins on a bus, and it was really nice being in their house, where we hadn't had a pillow fight or done anybodies poems, it was like I was good again. Jemima started telling Janiss pretty pig about what we did, she said "last night we did a big fight with . . ." but I stopped her, I said "Jemima come and look at this picture of a wale jumping out of the water."

When we finished our lessons and mum came to collect us she hardly looked at me, I just got a little kiss, so I thought "you are still cross." She said "we're just going to the house for a moment and then we're going to see Beppo because he's asked us over for dinner, isn't that nice?" Jemima said "oh yes, Beppo Beppo Beppo" but I thought "no it isn't nice, I don't want to go at all" but I couldn't do anything because I promised I'd be good, that was bad, that was awful.

Another awful thing happened when we were almost at Marther's house. Mum stopped and she said "Lawrence, Jemima, I want you to do me a favor, I want you to say your sorry about last night" and though she said both of us she only looked at me, I noticed it, so I thought "its like you are saying you are the really bad one Lawrence." Jemima didn't care, she said "oh yes" but I didn't want to at all, I just didn't, I looked at the house and I thought "I don't want to go in" but then I thought "but I promised."

They were all in the kitchen, Oska wasn't there, he was still busking, they were drinking wine, and mum sort of pushed us towards them, she said "Lawrence and Jemima have got something to tell you." Jemima said "sorry" she shouted it so loudly that Hilary laughed, and then they all looked at me, they were waiting. I thought "I wish we could just go back to those Vanhootins" but I made myself, I just did it, I said "I'm sorry about the pillow fight." I said it to Freddy Chrismas Bear because they were his poems, and he gave me a little smile, he said "that's okay Lawrence." Then Gus said "forget it kid" so I thought "you are nice after all, I'm sorry I made you a nasty dog." Hillery cow smiled too and even Martha gave me a look like she was saying "all right I suppose."

After that we went to Beppos. Mum said it wasn't that far so we walked. It was getting dark, I saw a shop selling postcards and I thought "I want to see those actually" so I went in, I just did it, mum and Jemima had to come after me, and then there was another shop with lots of glass bottles in different colors, so I went in there too, but then mum got annoyed, she said "stop daudeling Lawrence." After that we got to a square, there was a statue of a man in a big coat looking cross, and mum was looking at the map in her guidebook, she said "its somewhere round here" when suddenly I had a really good idea, because there was a stone bentch, I thought "I know, I'll go right to the end and then I'll jump off onto one leg, that will be good." But then d'you know what happened, I sort of fell down with a big crash so I thought "uhoh my leg really hurts now" and I sat down on the bench and I said "mum, I can't walk at all, I think its broken." Jemima got worried, she poked at my knee with her finger and said "will it come right off?" but mum wasn't nice at all, she said "I just haven't got time for this" and then she pulled my arm so I sort of had to walk, that was awfull, I thought "now everyone in this square will think I'm just stupid" I really hated that.

Then we went to Beppos. Beppo opened the door, he had funny hair, it was black with gray bits so it looked like someone on a ladder dropped paint on him, and he was very thin, he was a weasil. He and mum kissed their cheeks and I thought "I didn't like you even before when I never met you, and I really don't like you now" I thought "you made me look silly in the square." We sat down on sofas and I noticed there were some pictures on the walls, I thought "I know that one, its the colisseum" but it was the wrong color, it was red, and on the other wall there was the panthion but it was blue, so I thought "you have stupid pictures Beppo." But there was a lady there too, that was a surprise, Beppo said "this is Mariser who is from brazil, Mariser can you get us some olives?" and Mariser was very thin, she was pretty but cross, she was a cross otter. I thought "you don't want to get those olivs, you don't like us" I thought "but I'm glad you're here, Mariser, because then perhaps mum won't do Beppos ears after all."

I thought "I hope she won't, anyway" because mum was sitting next to him on the sofa and looking right at him like he was really interesting, it was like he was her favorite program on telly. She said "hows your wine collection going?" and he looked sad, he said "times are hard, Hannah, I had to sell it all" and mum frowned like this was terrible, she said "poor Beppo." Then I notised something, it was a big silver car on a shelf, so I thought "I bet that's heavy" I thought " I bet if you threw it it would really break something."

That was when Marisa said it was time for supper. I had an idea, I said "I have to go to the loo" but I didn't actually, I went back to the sitting room. I picked up the car and I was right, it was really heavy, but it had no floor with pipes and things underneath, it was just hollow, so I thought "this is a stupid car you've got Beppo, everyones feet will get scraped on the ground till theyre just bones." I looked round the room, there was a lamp shade and a funny animal on the floor, I think it was a lion, and a big table made out of glass. I made the car point at them all with its head lights, I went "vroom vroom" that was funny, but then I thought "all right mum" and I put it back on the shelf.

Dinner was lasanya, it was burnt, there were black bits, so I thought "I bet you did that on purpose, cross otter." Mum asked Beppo about the flat, she said "we'd just need it till the summer. So where is it?" and he said "its in Trastaveray" which mum really liked of course. He said "its my brothers flat actually" and mum said "how is Marco?" but Beppo looked cross like he ate a big piece of burnt lasanya, he said "he's doing pretty well, actually, he's in New York now, he's got his own gallery" which I knew, it's where you put pictures, I thought "why are you cross because Marcos got his gallery, don't you like pictures?" Then Beppo made a smily face like he was saying "I am such a nice kind weasil" and he said "I'm not really supposed to rent it out but I thought as your so desperete." Mum said "that's really nice of you, I'd love to see it" so when we finished our burnt supper we went to see the flat, we took a taxi. Mariser came too and I thought "thats good" I thought "you watch them, Mariser."

The flat was at the top of a big building so there were lots of stairs and as we went up I thought "actually it will be all right because I bet its horrible just like sneaky dolphins was, it will all just be a big waste of time." When we went in it was dark so Beppo had to switch on a light, but then he started opening the shutters, all the noise got in from the road, and suddenly I thought "actually this is a nice flat." It was really big you see, and it wasn't dirty or horreble, there were paintings on the walls of people in old clothes and when I looked out of a window I could just see a green tram going down the road with its lights, it went "ding ding ding" I thought "that's nice."

Mum was blinking and blinking, she said "oh and there's a little balconey, how lovely, and a washing machine too, that's so useful" she said "and it would be wonderful being here in Trasteveray" so I thought "she likes this flat" and Jemima was running up and down singing "itsey bitsy spider" so I thought "she likes it too." Then suddenly I thought "I don't like you Beppo but actually it would be really nice to have our own place, then we wouldn't have to stay with any more Cloudios or Marthers" I thought "the paintings are all high up, so Jemima won't be able to reck them" I thought "and I could get all my cars and Tintins back from Chrissy chicks" and I thought "I can always put a chair against the door to keep Beppo out."

Mum said "how long could we have it for?" and Beppo said "Marco probably won't come back before the summer, but if he does you'd have to move out straight away, you'd have to leave everything just like it was, then you could come back again when he's gone." Mum just nodded, she said "so how much d'you want?" and a funny thing happened, you see suddenly she wasn't looking like Beppo was her favorite program on the telly and he wasn't looking like he was the nicest, kindest weasil. So I thought "its like they were just pretending" I thought "you were just being nice to him because you wanted to get this flat, mum" I thought "I don't think you're going to do his ears after all" I thought "hurrah hurrah."

Beppo said it was such a lovely flat he could get lots for it if he put an advertisment in porter portaisey, he could get three thousand yuros. Then mum got annoyed, she said "but you can't put it in porta portaisey, Beppo, because your not supposed to be renting it out, remember." Beppo gave her a look like he thought "you are rude" he said "so how much d'you want to pay?" and mum said "five hundred." Now Beppo looked like this was a really silly joke, he said "all right you can have it for a thousand" and Mariser was watching them from the sofa, she was laughing like they were a really funny cartoon. I thought "uhoh, I bet that's too much for mum" I thought "but I really want to live here now, I don't want to go back to special monkeys." Mum shook her head, she said "five hundred is all I can pay, not a penny more, if its not enough then we'll just go right now."

Beppo didn't say anything, he didn't answewer at all, and then something bad happened. Mum got all our jackets and she put them on us really quick. Jemima giggeled, she didn't understand, and I gave mum a look, I was saying "no no, don't do this, I like it here" but she didn't take any notise. I thought "why didn't you ask us if we like this flat" I thought "you always ask us usually" but it was too late, because she was already pushing us through the door. Then there was a really strange thing. We were outside on the landing you see, we just started going down the stairs and I was thinking "oh no this is a pity" when suddenly Beppo came out after us and shouted "all right all right, you can have it."

I thought "oh yes, how amazing, hurrah" I thought "clever mum." We went down to the cash machine, mum got out her blue card and I thought "uhoh, I hope theres still some left" I thought "I wish I hadn't got that stupid radio controlled car" but there was enough actually, I thought "thank goodness." Beppo gave her the key and then he and Mariser went home, he said we mustn't break anything, especially the paintings.

So we went back up all the stairs, mum unlocked the door with her key and it felt really different now that Beppo and Mariser weren't there, because it was just ours now, it was so nice. I thought "hurrah hurrah, now we are real Romans" I thought "now we will really be safe."

CHAPTER FIVE

One day before I got the flu and dad came down from Scotland secretly, we were walking by the river near the cottege. It was really cold, there was a puddle with ice but it was holow, it was like glass with nothing underneath, so I jumped on it and broke it into little bits, that was fun. I said "mum, how come this puddles all frozen but the river is just water?" but she didn't ansewer, I don't think she heard me, actually, because she was looking at something up ahead, it was two bigger boys. I thought "what are they doing?" because they were throwing something and then suddenly mum shouted really loudly, it was like a scream, she said "stop that."

Then I saw what they were doing, because they were throwing little stones at a swan. When they saw mum they ran away but she ran after them, she was screeming so loud, I thought "you are really angry" she said "leave that poor thing alone." I looked at the swan but it was all right, actually, it was swimming along, it wasn't bleeding or dead or anything, it just looked cross. Then a funny thing happened because mum started crying, her face went red and I could see tears dribling down her face. Jemima looked all worried, so I said "what is it mum, the swans all right" but she said "I really just hate that. And the poor things all alone." Then she did a little smile, that was better, she crouched down and gave us a hug, she said "I'm so lucky, I've got you two, I don't need anybody else" and I laughed, I said "that's good, because we hardly know anybody else."

I think about that day sometimes, I don't really know why. I went right down to the edge of the water to be nice to the swan, I thought "mum will like that" but it just gave me a great big hiss and swam away.

I thought of my brilliant new plan just after we moved all our things into our new flat. Mum said we could have a treat to celebraite, just a little one, so we went to the toy shops in piatsa Navona. I got a Roman soldier, it wasn't an emperor because they didn't have any new ones and I didn't want two Julius Casaers, it was a gladiater, and Jemima got one too because she always wants what I have. Afterwards we went to a market so mum could look at all the vegetables, because she wanted to have a dinner party to say thank you to all her friends for helping us, she said "look at these oranges, aren't they amazing, you never see them big like this in rainy old England" and that was when I suddenly had my brilliant idea, I thought "I know, I will get lots and lots of roman solders so I have a whole army, I will get a fort and enemies so I can make real battles."

I told mum my idea but she just made a face, that was annoying, she said "Lawrence love, their eight yuros each, maybe you can have another one for easter." I said "but then I'll just have three, that's not an army at all." I thought "even if I can get Jemimas off her, if I can swop it for something, and even if she gets another one for easter and I swop that too, I'll still just have five, which isn't enough for a battle at all" but mum said "you've just had a big car, Lawrence, remember." After that we went to the supermarket and I went into a toy shop near it, I just ran in so mum and Jemima had to follow, but they only had three solders and they were just the same, they were eight yuros too, and Mum got a bit cross, she said "I told you, Lawrence, you can have one at easter."

When we got back there was a surprise. I saw her first, sitting at the café by our buildings door, I said "look mum, its Franseen." Franseen stood up, she smiled like she was a bit annoyed actually and she said "you never even told me you found a flat. Gus told me."

I thought "uhoh, please don't have a big argument you two, don't do your ray gun looks" and Jemima was watching too, but actually it was all right, mum said "we've only just moved in, Franseen." Then Franseen said "are you going to ask me up?" and mum said "of course." Franseen really liked it, she said "look at this, well done Beppo, I must ask if he has somewhere for me." I wanted her to stay, I wanted to show her my Julius Ceasaer and my new gladiator, but she said no, really she must go. Then she said "I brought you something" so I thought "oh good" and Jemima squealed and ran up to see. Mine was another hideous history, it was called Fanatical Fascists, I thought "I bet that's good" and Jemimas was a furry frog, when you pressed its tummy it did a croke. Then Franseen said a silly thing, she said "I wrote my telephone number in back of the book Lawrence, you know, just in case something goes wrong or someone gets lost" she said "its my sellphone so you can ring me anytime." I thought "that's nice but its silly" so I said "but we never get lost, mum has her guide book with maps" and I looked at mum, but she didn't say anything, she just sort of blinked.

ONE DAY THERE WAS a big fire in Rome, it went on for days, some people said Nero did it because he was emporer but nobody was sure. Thousands of famous temples and houses got burnt down and Nero went up a tower to watch, he said "doesn't it look beautifull" and then he sang a long song.

When the fire finished rome was all burnt, there were just little black pieces of stone and wood, even Nero's palace was burnt down, so he was really sad, he said "oh no, this is dreadfull, where will I live now." Then he decided "I know, I will build myself a new palace and it'll be much better this time, it will be huge" and that's what he did. It was the biggest palace in the world, it took years and it was called Neros golden House, theres still a bit left but you have to ring up and book and we never remembered. It was so big that there were arcades you could walk along for miles, there was a lake that was like the sea, there were huge gardens and forests. There were bathrooms with special different taps so you got seawater, or water with sulfer in it, that is yellow and smells horreble, and there were dining rooms with cielings that went round and round so flowers fell on your head. When you went in there was a huge room with a statue a hundred and twenty feet high, it was of Nero.

When everything was finished and the builders went home Nero took all his things to his new palace, he arranged them nicely and then he asked all his freinds round for supper. He walked all round his new palace and he felt so happy, he smiled and smiled, he said "thank goodness, at last now I have my own place again, isn't it lovely" he said "now everything will be all right."

The next day was Sunday and we went to Ikeyer which was miles away, so we went in the car, it was because mum said it was very cheap. I said "will they have roman solders there?" and mum said "we'll just have to wait and see." Ikeyer was huge, it was like an air port, but they didn't have anything, they just had lots of tables and cubords etc and some balls and big green snakes and plastic tents, they didn't have any roman solders at all. A man tried to rob mum again, he started unziping her hand bag when she was looking at forks but he ran away when mum screemed and after that we got Jemimas bed, which was why we went to Ikeyer actually, because she didn't have one in our flat you see, she was still just in mums bed. The bed came in big card board boxes that were really heavy, mum said you had to put it together yourself, it cost sixty yuros and mum said it was a real bargin, so I said "mum when we get back home can I have roman solders that cost sixty yuros, that will be fair" but mum got really annoyed, she said "Jemima needs a bed, you've already got one, now stop it Lawrence."

When we drove back I thought "I wonder what I can do?" I thought "Peter Norris does a paper round, he gets up really early in the morning and goes on his bicycle but mum says he is much too young and anyway Rome is all just flats and I don't have a bicicle." When we got back and stopped the car mum said she couldn't carry Jemimas bed because it was too heavy, she said "I don't know how I'm going to do this" but fortunately just then a man with a tiny beerd like a triangle parked his motor bike and he helped us, he carried the really heavy box up the stairs. I helped with the other one, I held the end, and as we were going up I had another really good idea, I thought "oh yes hurrah, that's the answer."

I told it to mum when we went back down, we had to hurry because mum blocked another car, we could hear it honking, I said "I want to swop my new radio controled car for lots of Roman solders." But mum didn't like my new idea, she said "this really isn't the time Lawrence, and anyway they won't take it back now, we threw away the box remember, they'd only take it back if it didn't work." I thought about that, and then as we drove round and round looking for a parking place I had another idea. When we got back to the flat I gave Hermann his new water and nuts and then I looked everywhere until I found a screw driver, it was in a drawer in the kitchen, and I unscrewed the radio controlled car really carefully, I opened it up like it was a big mouth. Then I got some scissors and cut a little red wire and it worked, when I screwed it all together again it didn't work at all, I moved the control stick but it didn't do anything. Mum said "that was a really stupid thing to do" but I thought "you just wait mum."

Then a funny thing happened. I thought "what will I do now, I know, I will read my new Hidious History, Fanatical Fashists" but I couldn't find it. It wasn't in the sitting room or my bedroom or anywhere. I asked mum and she helped look, but we still couldn't find it, and then she said "unless it dropped in the trash can by mistake." I thought "uhoh, of course" because I often worry about that actually, because once the garbagemen take it away its lost forever, because they will put it in a huge field full of millions and millions of bags of rubbish, they will never remember where they put yours. So I went really quickly into the kitchen to look in the garbage bag but there was hardly anything, it was just egg shells and things. Mum frowned and said "actually I took out a bag last night" so we all went down stairs, Jemima came too so she wouldn't be left behind, but there weren't any garbage bags at all, they were gone.

That was sad. I said "my lovely new hideous history, and I never read any of it." Mum was nice, we started going back up the stairs and she said "don't worry Lawrence, I'll get you another one." Jemima was silly, she said "and can I have another frog" which wasn't fair at all, because she still had her frog, it didn't get thrown away, but I didn't take any notice, I said "we can ask Franseen where the shop is where she got it when she comes to our dinner" because that was all arranged now, it was going to happen the day after tomorrow, mum already asked her friends and they all said they were coming. But then mum was just unlocking our door with her key when she said a funny thing, she sort of said it into the door, she said "Franseen isn't coming."

That was strange. I said "why not, mum, is she ill?" but mum said "no, there just aren't enough chairs." I said "but we have to ask Franseen, mum, because she's really nice, she let us stay in her flat and gave me and Jemima all those things" and Jemima said "yes yes, Franseens nice" but it didn't work. Suddenly Mum looked really cross, she goes like that sometimes, her voice went really loud and she said "didn't you hear what I said, there aren't enough chairs? We'll just have to ask her another time" and I almost said "no you have to ask her now, mum, you must" but I didn't in the end, I just didn't feel like it.

THE NEXT MORNING MUM WOKE us up early so we could go to the market and get food for the dinner. She said "tell me, lesonfon, is there anything special you want me to make? You have to tell me right now." Jemima jumped up and down, she said "I want a pink cake" which was stupid actually, so I told her "don't be silly Jemima, because that is for babies, this is a grown up dinner" but mum said "no, we can have that" and I got a bit annoyed, I thought "mum always does what Jemima says, its not fair" so I said "I want chicken with black sauce" but mum just laughed, she said "I'll see what I can do."

We went to the market, we bought all the things, and mum said "the vegtable lady wasn't very friendly today" and I said "perhaps she was just really busy" and Jemima said "she was nice, she gave me my apple" but mum said "the cheese man wasn't friendly either" though I thought he was all right, I said "he said chow bella."

After that we took everything back home and then Jemima

and me went to the Vanhootins. That was annoying actually, because I wanted to do my new plan, but then it was all right after all, because mum wasn't late from work this time, she said "I need to get a few things from a shop just across the river" so I thought "oh good, hurrah" and I said "is it near the piazzer Navona, because then I can take my radio controlled car back." Mum just looked at me, she said "you are a real pest sometimes Lawrence" but we went anyway. We had to go home first to get the car, mum said "this is just ridiculous" and d'you know it worked. I cleaned the wheels so it didn't look like I drove it round and round the fountain, I said it just broke down, and though the man was really suspicious, he looked at the car and tried to make it go, he changed the batteries and then he looked at mums riseet again and again, in the end he said "all right" quite crossly.

So I got twelve new solders and a catapult, I already had two of course, which meant if I got Jemimas off her I would have fifteen. I thought "hurrah, this is a really good army" I thought "if I get another one at easter and I get Jemimas easter one too I will have seventeen." Only one solder was an enemy. Mum said the romans worst enimy was the Germans but they didn't have any left so I got a Swiss Guard instead. He had a helmet and clothes with lots of colors, mum said they guard the pope, she said he would be fine because the Swiss are right next to Germany, they are almost the same, he was holding a spear with an ax on the end.

After that we went home, and when we were walking down our street mum said "oh look, that yellow car, I notised it there before" so I said "that's not like dads either, its too small" and

mum said "I know Lawrence love" but she looked in the windshield and then up at the building above it, which was flats just
like ours. Then Jemima did a kind of jumping dance, she sang
"yellow car, yellow car" like it was a song, she is so silly, I got so
annoyed, I said "shhhh Jemima, just shut up."

When we got home I showed Hermann all my new roman
soldiers and I think he liked them too, he poked his nose through
the bars. Then we did lots of cooking for the meal. Mum made
red sauce for the spaggeties, it was tomato, she made lots in a big
pot, it smelt really nice, and we helped, I peeled all the onions
even though they made me cry, I said "what about the black
sauce?" and mum said "we'll do that tomorrow." After that we
made Jemimas pink cake, Jemima and me poured lots of things
in the mixture and mum let us lick the spoons, then she did the
pink iceing, she said "we'll put in the strawberries and cream
tommorow."

That night I couldn't sleep. There was a big thunder storm
with lots of rain so it sounded like there was something really
heavy like a steam roller on the roof, there was thunder and lightning. Hermann was going round and round in his wheel, I think
he was a bit frightened, actually, so I went up to his cage and wispered "its all right Hermann, its just thunder" and actually I
didn't need to wisper I think, because Jemima didn't wake up
even when the thunder was so loud it made me jump, mum says
she would sleep through an earth quake. I kept thinking about
my soldiers, I had them all in a neet line on the shelf and I kept
looking at them, even though it was hard to see them in the dark,
they were just like sort of black lines. I thought "they are really

really good" I thought "tomorrow I will build the fort, I will tell mum I need some gray paint, I will make it out of cardbord from serial packets, it will have towers and a flag and it will be just like a real fort, I will show all mums friends when they come." I could imagine every bit of it, there were doors and a draw bridge, it was amazing. I decided "I will put the enemy in the fort and then Julius Caesaer will shout 'now' and all the romans will attack, they will fire stones with the catapult and some will sneak up from the side so the enemy won't see."

I was still thinking about my fort when I heard footsteps going past outside the bedroom door. I thought "the thunderstorm has woken mum up and now shes going to the loo" which she does in the night sometimes, but then a strange thing happened. Eventually the thunderstorm stopped you see, it just went drip instead, but I then heard mum walking past again so I thought "she just went to the loo, wheres she going now?" After that she came back again so I thought "she is going to bed now, thats all right" but then she was walking again, actually it was almost like she was running, her feet were going so fast, they went "tap tap tap," that was funny. I thought "what are you doing mum?" I thought "I will lisen really carfully to see what you do next" but I don't remember anything after that, so I think I just fell asleep.

When I woke up the sun was shining on the floor in a thin line, it was warm and something was strange, something was wrong, I didn't know what. Jemima was still sleeping, I thought "you big lazy bones" and I got out of bed. Mum was in the sitting room, she was in her dressing gown, she had a chair but she wasn't sitting in it, she was standing and looking out of the window like there was something really intresting out there. I said "what are you looking at, mum?" and she jumped a bit, she gave me a cross look and said "Lawrence, you scared me" and that was when I realized what was funny. Everything was quiet you see, there weren't lots of cars, and the sun was really warm, so I looked at the clock and I was right, it said "ten oh five." I said "mum, why didn't you wake us up, its really late, what about the Vanhootins and your job?" Mum gave me a funny look, she sort of blinked, and she said "lets just stay here today, Lawrence love, I think its going to rain."

The window was open and I could hear a man shouting "percay" which means "why." I thought "theres a little cloud over there but mostly it is nice, its a lovely sunny day, I don't think it will rain and usually mum doesn't mind getting wet anyway." I said "but you have to go to work, mum, the cristians will be cross." Mum frowned like she had a headake, she didn't say anything, I thought "she's not going to answer me, shes not going to talk at all," and then I thought of something else, I said "and what about your diner." But mum just shook her head like I hadn't listened to her, she said "I think perhaps we should do that another time."

Now I thought "what will I do?" I thought "probably it is too late for the cristians and the Vanhootins because Jemima is still in dreamland, we aren't dressed and we haven't even had our breakfast" but I thought "but we have to do the diner party, if we don't then everything will go bad, I just know it." So I said "but you've asked them all, you promised, and I was really looking forward to it" which was true actually, I wanted to show them all my new solders. Mum made her headache face but I thought "oh no you don't" and I was really quick, I said something I don't say to mum, even if she has gone funny I don't say it, I just don't like to, I thought "I will just try" so I said "mum, are you all right?" She gave me a look so I thought "uhoh it's not working" but then she said "I'm fine Lawrence, don't be silly" so I said "then lets do the diner party" and d'you know it worked, mum closed her eyes like I was a really big pest but she said "all right all right we'll have the dam thing" so I thought "that's good."

After that everything was a bit better. Mum rang the Vanhootins and her cristians to say we werent coming today, she said Jemima had a bad nose bleed which was a lie of course, and the Vanhootins didn't mind but the cristians were annoyed just like I thought, they told mum "all right just this once." Jemima woke up, we had breakfast and we went out to go shopping, but on the stairs mum kept stopping and sort of looking round the corner, that was funny, it was like she was scared, so I thought "who are you frightened of mum, is it Chintsier and Gabrielley, is it Beppo, does his brother want his flat back?" Eventually we got all the rest of the food for the diner, so I said "mum, can we go and get some gray paint now, I need it for my fort" but she got cross, she said "no we have to hurry up and get all the food ready" that was a shame.

So we did the strawberries and cream in Jemimas pink cake, and then mum did another cake which was choclate. After that we did the chicken too, mum did a sauce with mushrooms, and I said "but that's not black that's brown" but mum said "its near enough." When we finished the potatoes I thought "there's a bit of time left, I can still do a little bit on my fort, I can make a start" but then mum said "Lawrence, can you help me clear up the sitting room." So we moved all the chairs, mum put lots of plates and glasses on the table, she said "they'll just have to help themselves and eat it on their laps" and I thought "doesn't it look beautifull."

After that mum put on new clothes and they all started arriving. The doorbell rang again and again, Jemima tried to get it but I was quicker, so I never did do my fort in the end, but I didn't mind, actually, I just thought "hurrah, it's a party." First it was the Vanhootins, and they really liked our flat, everybody did actually, Bill vanhootin said "these paintings are quite something." After that it was mum's cristians, and they weren't cross any more that mum didn't go to work today, they said "what a wonderful cooking smell" so I thought "I really must give you your animals now, you cristians" but there wasn't time, because more people kept coming.

It was Crissy, she gave mum a big hug and then she said "is Franseen here yet?" and mum gave her a look, she said "she's not coming actually" so I thought "uhoh" but it was all right, because then the door bell went again and it was Marther special monkey's house, all five of them. They really liked our flat too, Gus said "you jamy beggars" and Freddy chrismas bear said "a penthouse of wonders." Then suddenly I looked all round and I thought "what a lot of people there are in our flat, isn't it amazing, its like we are in a train."

Though I hadn't done my fort I showed Crissy chick my roman solders, I told them I was going to make a fort later, and she said "how lovely." Then I showed Hermann to Tina mouse and Leonora bossy rabbit, I let them hold him for a bit and they really liked him, they said "hes so cute" and then I showed them all our toys to cheer them up and they said "wow you've got lots of leggo." After that I showed them how we could make lots of things like cars and airoplanes, not just walls, and I showed them my tintins but they could only look at them a bit because mum came in and said dinner was ready.

Everybody said mums pasta with tomato sauce was really delicious, I had seconds, then I had chicken too, I scraped off all the mushroom sauce because I don't like that, and though it was on my lap so I had to be really careful I only spiled a tiny bit, it didn't go on the carpet. Janniss pretty pig made everyone say "cheers" she said "heres to the cook, heres to Hannah" and mum was smiling like she might go "pop" she wasn't sad at all any more, so I thought "that's good, shes all right now."

After that we had the cakes, everybody liked them too, but then Crissy and mums cristians said they had to go home now, so I thought "no don't go yet, please don't go because this is all so nice, why can't you stay." Jemima fell asleep on the sofa so mum put her to bed, and then the Vanhootins all went too, that was a shame, which just left Marthers ones. They stayed a bit, Gus opened some more wine, which was nice even though they weren't my favorites, I thought "my favorites are Crissy chick and the Vanhootins I think." But then they all got up too, Hillary nice cow said "I brought you some jinger biscuits I made" I tried one and it was nice, you had to chew it really hard. Freddy Chrismas bear gave mum a poem on a piece of paper, it was about the

moon going up into the sky above rome and watching all the people eating dinner and drinking wine and driving on their motor
bikes, mum said "oh freddy, how lovely." Marther special monkey
said "you must all come over to dinner really soon, come next
week" and Gus was funny, he said "no come tommorow, actually
come right now" and Oska did his funny face like he was going
"pling pling" because he didn't have his giutar of course, he left
it at home, but everyone laughed anyway.

So we shut the front door and suddenly the flat was really
quiet and empty, it felt all sad. Mum started clearing up all the
plates and things and she looked tired so I said "I'll help you
mum" but she said "no Lawrence love, you go to bed, its really
late" so I did. I got into my pijamas, I brushed my teeth and I said
good night. Then I lay in bed, I could hear mum doing washing
up in the kitchen, and I thought "mum should let me help, actually, because I cant go to sleep at all because I am so excited" I
thought "I bet I'll be awake all night, I bet I'll be awake till
dawn" I thought "I must remember to tell mum we must have
another dinner party like that really soon."

SUDDENLY IT WAS DARK and someone was shaking my arm so I
thought "whats happening?" She was wispering "Lawrence wake
up, please wake up" and it was mum, I could see her face from the
light that came round the curtin and her eyes looked funny, it
was like she was scared but she was all excited. I thought "uhoh,
whats this?" She said "we mustn't wake Jemima, something's
happened" so I got out of bed quietly, I followed her out, and I

was thinking "I wonder what it is, is it a burgler or did something get broken, was it one of the pictures of people in old cloths? Or did somebody ring up from england, did the cottage get burnt down?" But it wasn't any of these things at all actually. We went to the kitchen, the light was really bright so my eyes went blink, then mum opened the fridge and took out one of the cakes that we had for pudding, it was Jemimas pink one, there was just a big slice left, and mum said "look."

I looked but I couldn't see anything, it just looked like cake, so I said "what is it, I don't understand." Mum pointed at it again and this time I notised that there were some tiny red spots, I didn't see them before, so I said "what are they mum, are they juice from the strawberries?" but mum shook her head, she looked sort of sad now, she was holding the cake and she was looking at the floor. She said "smell it, Lawrence love, its poisson."

I didn't understand. I smelt it and I thought "actually it does smell a bit funny I suppose." I said "what d'you mean?" and then mum started crying a bit, she said "Lawrence love, I'm so sorry, the last thing I wanted is to scare you with all of this but I'm so worried, I found out yesterday but I didn't want to tell you, actually I didn't want to believe it myself. But you have to know, for your own safety. Your fathers here in Rome. He's followed us. Its so awful. Just when we've finally got everything sorted out this happens."

I could hear a car go beep somewhere, it was quiet so I thought "that cars a long way away" and then I thought "here I am with mum by the fridge in the middle of the night" I don't know why I thought that. I looked at the red spots and I thought "if I eat those will I die?" and suddenley I wanted to touch them, that was stupid, I knew I couldn't really. I thought "so that was why she kept stopping and looking round the corner when we went down the stairs, she was watching for dad." I felt like my arms went all heavy, I thought "this is dreadfull, we came all the way here to be safe and now we aren't after all" and suddenley I got angry, I thought "why does he have to follow us everywhere like this, why does he have to put poison on the cake and spoil everything every time." I thought "I really hate him" I thought of his face with his hair that went up like smoke and I wanted to hit it hard so it was just gone, it was all smashed away to nothing. But then a funny thing happened, I thought "wait a minute" and I said "but he cant be, mum, he doesn't even know we're here."

Now mum was exited again, she wasn't crying any more, she wiped her nose with a paper hankercheef, her eyes were all quick and looking and she said "just come over here." We went into the sitting room to a window, I thought "is he down there in the road?" but when I started looking out of the window she stopped me, she said "be careful Lawrence love" and she just let me look round the edge. She said "over there, d'you see?" It was another big building down the road a bit, it was just like ours, I didn't understand. Mum said "you see those windows at the top, the shutters were all closed before, now they're open, he's in there, he's watching us. I saw him, I'm sure of it. That was last night, but it was just the same. The shutters were shut during the day but open in the evening."

I said "are you sure it was him?" and mum gave me a look

like I was being so stupid but she didn't want to get cross, she said "don't you remember the car, the yellow car, it was parked just below there." I thought "but mum . . ." I said "that wasn't his car, it was different" but she said "of course it wasn't his, but he always likes that color, don't you see, so he hired that one when he flew here. I bet he came with rianair, they come from scotland now, I saw it on a poster." I said "but you still haven't told me, mum, how would he know we're here in Rome?"

Now mum got annoyed, her arms went in the air like she was throwing up little balls and she said "Franseen of course. She told him. Haven't you noticed how strange she's been to us. She really hates me, I know it." Then she wispered. "I never told you this, Lawrence, because I didn't want to upset you, but all those years ago when I lived here, Franseen really liked your father." I said "you mean she wanted to get married to him?" and mum said "that's right. So that's why she wants to hurt us, d'you see, she hates me because I got away from him, because I got us all away, they both do."

I didn't know, actually. I thought "mum is clever" I thought about Franseen cat liking dad years ago, I thought "go away cat, leave him alone" but then I thought "but Franseens nice, she gave me my hideous histeries." And then suddenly I thought of something else, I thought "oh yes, hurrah" I thought "why didn't I think of that before, thats silly" I thought "we're safe after all" so I said "but mum, he can't have poissoned the cake, because the front doors locked, remember, he can't get in." But Mum didn't look pleased like I thought, that was a pity, she just shook her head and said "it was Beppo, Lawrence love, can't you see. Beppo gave him the key. Beppo would do anything for money." She said "your father must have been here for days. That's how he's already been turning people against us, like the woman in the market."

Suddenly I felt all sort of tired, like all the breathe went out of me. I thought "it was all so nice, and now its broken." I think mum saw, because she looked sad again, she closed her eyes and said "I'm so sorry about all of this, Lawrence. I really shouldn't have told you, I tried not to, but I was so worried, I thought you just had to know." Then everything went quiet, mum was looking at me, so I thought "now she is waiting" and d'you know I couldn't think what to say. It was like all my thoughts went somewhere else and there was just an empty space.

I didn't want to make mum worse, I didn't mean to, I thought "I must help her" but it was like it didn't work. I thought "I want to go back to bed" and then suddenly I just said it, I didn't mean to, it was like an acident, I said "but Franseens always really nice." That was wrong, mum looked surprised like I hit her. She said "he could come back at any moment, for goodness sake Lawrence, I really need your help." I tried to get scared, I really did, but somehow it all went wrong again, so I said "its really late mum, hes probably gone to bed" and she turned away, she frowned like she had her headacke, she said "what d'you think, should we put a chair against the door?"

She was waiting again. I thought "why are you asking me, mum, you usually do the chair against the door, you don't ask me" so I said "I don't know, I suppose so" and d'you know that was what got her really angry, it was funny, I only said "I don't know I suppose so." She gave me a look like I was horreble, like

I was a really bad boy, and she said "all right then I'll just do it myself." So she went off with a kind of thumping walk and got a chair from the dining room and I tried to help her, I tried to carry one of its legs, but it was too late, she wouldn't let me now, she lifted it high up so I had to let go, actually it hurt my hand a bit but I didn't say anything. Then she put it against the front door and walked off, she didn't look at me at all.

I thought "all right then, mum, I'll just go to bed then, it's the middle of the night isnt it." But it was hard to sleep, I could hear Jemima breathing and then I heard mum walking about, she went past again and again so I thought "shes not tired" her feet went "tap tap tap tap" really fast so it was like she was in a race.

WHEN EMPORERS DIED they got made into Gods but only if they were good and everybody liked them. Caligula was bad and nobody liked him so one day he thought "I know, I won't wait until I'm dead, I will make myself into a god right now."

So he told everybody "I am a god actually" and he made his servants build a new temple. They made a statue out of gold and put it inside, it looked like Caligula, it was just the same size and every morning his servants dressed it up in the same cloths he was wearing that day. After that Caligula said "everybody can come and wership me now" and lots of people did, it was so he wouldn't execute them. Caligula was really pleased, he thought "I like being a god" and he started talking to all the other gods because he was just the same as them now, he talked to their statues in their temples. Sometimes he was cross with them, he shouted "I will get you for that" and sometimes they were his friends. His best freind was a god called Jupiter and Caligula liked him so much that he built a little house right next to Jupiters temple so he could go and stay with him sometimes.

After that Caligula decided that now he was a god everything had to be really special, it had to be just what a god would do. He had his bath in oil that was really expensive and for his supper he had pearls that were melted down in viniger, or special meat and vegtables that were all colored gold. I don't know what they tasted like, probably they were a bit funny but Caligula didn't mind as long as it was real gold gods food. Then he thought "wait a minute, what about my holidays, what does a god do for that?" so he got his servants to build him a boat which was enormous like a palace, it had thousands of slaves to push the oars, it had jewels stuck on the outside, it had a huge bath, it even had a col-lonnade where you could go for a nice walk. Calligula sat down on a special sofa on the boat, he listened to singers singing him lovely music and he watched the land go past far away, and he thought "oh yes, this is good, this is right, now I really am a proper god."

But there was a strange thing. Even though Caligula was like a proper god and did all his gods things, he still got really scared. When there was a big storm with thunder and lightning he hid under his blanket because it made him jump. Sometimes he got worried that Germans would invade Rome, he thought "oh no, they will come and get me" though of course this was impossible because there were no Germans for hundreds of miles and the Ro-man army was really strong, it would defeat them. Most of all he was scared that someone would sneak up and assasinate him, which was possible, actually, because everybody hated him. So he had thousands of people executed so they couldn't assassinate him, it was just in case.

Often he couldn't sleep at all, he lay awake for hours, he thought "its boring lying here." He got headaches which were really bad, he said "I feel all confused" he thought "I don't know whats happening." So he decided "I know, I will go to the seaside, that will help clear my head." But it didn't work. So poor god Caligula executed more and more people, he went to the seaside again and again, but it didn't help at all, his head just got worse and worse.

When I woke up I could hear the cars were quiet and the sun was hot which meant we hadn't gone to the Vanhootins again, mum hadn't gone to her job, so I thought "uhoh, those cristians will be really cross now." I could hear mum and Jemima outside, Jemima said "I don't want that one, I want my red dress" but I just stayed in bed, I didn't want to get up, I thought "I just don't feel like it." The shutters were open a bit so I could look out and see some sky and a roof, I thought "I wonder if dads in his build-ing, I wonder if hes watching us" I thought "he might be." I thought "what will I tell Hermann?" but I couldn't think of any-thing, so I just said "hello Hermann."

A bit later the door opened and mum looked in, she was still cross, I could see it. She said "hurry up Lawrence, we're going out to get some breakfast at a café." I thought "that's strange, why does she want to go outside to a café when shes worried dads out there?" But then when I got up I saw there were two garbage bags by the door and I understood, I thought "oh yes of course, mum has thrown away all our food in case its poissoned, so we have to go out." I thought "I hope it really is poissoned or thats a big waste of food" but I didn't say anything, I didn't want to make mum crosser. I decided "I will just stay really quiet today, I will be like a mouse, it will be like I'm hardly here at all, then everything will be all right."

Mum rang up someone, I think it was her bank again, she said "no I can't come in and see you, I already told you that" so I thought "uhoh mum" I thought "you shouldn't have annoyed your cristians like that, they won't pay you now I bet." Then we went out, mum took both the garbage bags, she didn't even ask me, and on the stairs she kept stopping and looking round the corner. I thought "I know why you are doing that now, mum" and then a funny thing happened, because Jemima noticed too, she said "what are you looking for mum?" so I thought "what will you say now, what will you tell her?" and mum said "I'm just checking everything's all right, lamikin, I'm just checking there isn't a big dog or something." That was a big lie of course, and it was a mistake, actually, because Jemima is really frightened of dogs, even silly little ones like chiwawas, so she said "I want you to carry me mum" which mum couldn't do because of the garbage bags, so she made me stay with Jemima while she took them down, but then Jemima was a cry baby, she shouted "mummy mummy, what about the big dog, it will bite you." I told her "stop it Jemima, there isn't any dog, you silly" but it didn't help, she kept shouting until mum ran back up again.

Outside in the road I could see mum looking up at dads building, actually she was watching everywhere, her eyes were pointing like arrows. I looked for the yellow car but it was gone, so I thought "perhaps he has hidden it now." I thought "is dad suddenly going to come out of his buildings door right now?" I thought "is he going to jump out of that green tram, is he going to run out of that choclate shop" I thought "that will be really really bad" but he didn't, and then somehow I couldn't quite think it any more, I just kept forgeting, I thought "I wonder what crusson will I have, will I have jam or cremer?" We had to eat our breakfast really fast because mum got annoyed, she said "hurry up you two, we've got so much to do" and then in the end she got fed up and just pushed us out of the door, she said "you can finish your crussons on the way" but Jemima dropped hers on the pavment so we had to go back and get another one.

Then a funny thing happened. Mum went to the bank machine, I thought "that won't work I bet" but then she opened her purse and she undid a zip, I think it was a secret part, because she took out a new card, I never saw it before, it was brown. I said "that's new mum" but she just frowned, she pressed all the buttons really carefully and it worked, I think she got quite a lot of money actually, I only saw it for a moment because she put it into her purse but they were orange which are bigger than red or blue ones, they are fifties. Jemima tried to see too, she jumped up and down, but then mum gave us a look, she said "don't get any ideas, this really has to last. And then I have to think of some way to pay it all back."

After that we went to the supermarket, Jemima sat in the cart like she always has to, and we were both saying "I want strawber-

ries" or "I want that serial because I never had that one before."
Usually mum gets things we ask for, some of them anyway, but
this time she just got cross, she said "lisen you two, what did I
just say, I told you we have to make this money last." So we just
got lots of really borring things, it was spaggetties and tins of
tomatos and vegetables like onions, because mum said she was
going to make a really big sauce, and she got some funny milk in
blue boxes which she said you don't have to put in the fridge, she
got lots of oranges and tangerines but she wouldn't get any cherries, she said "they cost a fortune."

I thought "I wonder if there were cherries in that garbage bag
you threw away" I thought "if our food wasn't poissonned after all
then we could have spent this money on roman solders, I would
have a really huge army now, and roman solders are much better
than food, actually, because they last forever" but I didn't say anything, I was still keeping quiet, I just said "don't forget to get
more nuts for Hermann." I carried two bags and mum carried
two and she kept shouting "Jemima hold on to my fingers, I said
hold on to my fingers" which was because she was worried
Jemima would run off the pavement and get squoshed by a car,
or dad would jump out and get her, but he didn't actually.

After that we went to the lock shop, mum showed the man
her key and they talked in Italian, mum said "god, I didn't think
it would cost that much." Then she and the man went and looked
at bolts, which are big metal things which you pull out across
the door, and the man said "pomedridgeo" which I knew actually,
because siniora Morrow did that, it means "afternoon." Mum
opened her purse and she got out her blue card, she looked at it

159

for a bit, but then she put it back and she paid with her new yuro notes, there were still quite a lot left I think.

When we were going I thought "I will ask now" so I said "can we go to a paint shop now, mum, because I need some gray paint for my fort that I'm going to make" but mum said "not now Lawrence, we have to get all this food in the fridge." I thought "I don't care actually" I thought "I will make my fort anyway, the writing on the serial packet will just be grafeety, because my calamitous casears book said the romans had lots of grafeety." So I started, I did it in the sitting room, I brought Hermann over in his cage so he could watch, but he was asleep. I took the serial in its bag out of the packit, I thought "oh yes, this is really big, it will make a really good fort" but then when I started cutting it up it sort of went all smaller, I thought "I hope I've got enough selotape."

That was when the telephone rang. Mum said "hello, hello?" like there was nobody there, but she did a strange thing, I noticed it, Jemima didn't because she was busy trying to take her dolls dress off, which she couldn't because it was the cloth doll she got when I got my electric car and the cloths were all sewn on, that was silly. What mum did was she pulled the telephone plug right out of the wall. She did it quickly but I saw because roman phone plugs are really big you see, they are gray and round like half a tomato. I thought "why are you saying 'hello hello' mum, because you know you can't hear anything because you just pulled out the plug." I thought "nobody will be able to ring us now" but I didn't say anything, I just didn't feel like it, I did my fort.

I finished the tower, it was a bit wobbly but I thought "its not so bad". Then I went and looked for more boxes. One was biscuits, I put them all in a bowl, and another was for pasta, it was smaller but I thought "its still a box" so I put the pasta in another bowl, I thought "I wish we hadn't thrown away all the boxes for Jemimas bed, because they were really huge." Then I made the other tower, Jemima fell asleep, I ran out of selotape but I found a stapler with lots of staples, I joined the towers together with a wall, but the new one was wobbly too, and the writing didn't really look like grafeety even though it was upside down, it just looked like biscuit and pasta box writing. I tried to put the swiss guard on the tower but he kept falling over, it was because the roof wasn't straight, and I was still trying to fix it when mum came in. I said "this forts really difficult, mum" and she said "Lawrence, come with me, theres something you need to see."

I thought "what is it now, I hope we don't have to throw away all our new food again." I thought "I hope shes not cross because I took the boxes and put the pasta and biscuits in bowls." But she didn't take me to the kitchen, instead she took me into my and Jemimas bedroom, so I thought "I hope my roman solders are all right" but they were all still there in their line on the shelf. Mum took me over to my bed and she said "I was just making it and . . ." Then she lifted up the doovay and d'you know what was under it, that was a big surprise, I could hardly believe it, I thought "how did they get there?" Because you see there in my bed were two nives from the kitchen, I recognized them, they were the little sharp ones that mum used for chopping onions and carrots and things.

I said "I don't understand." Mum gave me a look like I said

something stupid or got a math sum wrong but she didn't mind, she said "he must have come in this morning when we were out at the shops." I looked at them and then I reached out and touched one, I don't know why I did that, I knew it was real of course, the metel bit was cold. I thought "I didn't put them here, Jemima didn't, because she was always with me" I thought "mum wouldn't put them here."

Then a funny thing happened, it was like a big door opened and suddenly I could see right in. I thought "so mum's right." And d'you know I could feel it now, it was like it was in my stomach, I thought "he really is in his building watching us" I thought "he did get in last night and poisson the cake" I thought "he was out there this morning, he might have jumped out of that green tram." Suddenly I felt all shivery, I thought "he was here in our flat when we were having our breakfast at the café" I thought "what if mum hadn't noticed, then we would have eaten that cake, we would have got poisoned, I would have just got into bed and got stabed."

I felt so angry. I thought "how dare you dad." I looked at mum but she wasn't sad, that was good, she wasn't squeezing her hair or scratching her hands, she was just watching me with her serious look, she was waiting, so I said "I really hate him." Then a funny thing happened, she sort of closed her eyes and she gave me a hug, she said "Lawrence love, we're going to be all right. All that matters is that we're together." That was good, that was nice, I thought "yes we can do this, actually its just like before" so I said "we mustn't tell Jemima because she is too young to understand" and mum said "your right, Lawrence." I said "we'd better put them away before she wakes up" so we got all the nives and put them back in the kitchen in the drawers.

I thought "what will we do now? We must make a plan." I said "let's check our food" and I counted it all, I said "this will last for ages but we'll still have to be carefull, we mustn't eat too much for our supper" and mum said "okay Lawrence" then she said "perhaps we should have a good look round the flat, so we know just what's here." So we did that, we looked in all the rooms, but we didn't find any more food except a few tins of tomatoes. But then mum said "how about up there?" and she pointed at the cieling, because there was a little door in it, mum said it was a hatch. She said "I think I'll have a look" so she put the table under it and then she put a chair on the table and climbed up.

I said "be careful mum" but she didn't fall down, she pushed the hatch so it opened and then she pulled herself up so she disappeared, even her feet. That was funny, I climbed on the table and I said "what is it mum, is there more food?" because I could hear her scraping lots of things around, and she said "nothing like that" so I thought "thats a shame" but then there was a surprise. Suddenly there was a bang and a big empty cardbord box fell right down on the table beside me, and then two more as well. Mum was looking down out of the hatch and she was holding a tin, she said "look what I found." I didn't understand, I said "what is it mum" and she laughed, she said "paint you silly, we can make a new fort." It wasn't grey, it was cream, mum said it was for the walls, but that was all right, I thought "oh yes, hurrah."

So we started the new fort. Hermann woke up now so he

watched through the bars. Mum said this time we must do a plan first, she found some paper and a pencil and she did a picture, shes really good at drawing actually, it had four towers and four walls holding them together, there was a flag. I thought "these boxes are much bigger than the serial box, and the card board is much thicker too" I thought "this fort will be amazing like the one I thought about in the night" and that was when I heard the doorbell ring. At first I didn't think anything, I just thought "I wonder who that is" but then I suddenly remembered.

I looked at mum and the smile she had from drawing the fort all went away, it was like someone just switched it off, her eyes went blink blink and she started touching the back of her hand with her finger nails. I looked out of the window at dads building and the shutters were still open, but then I thought "that doesn't mean he's still in there." I said "what if its not him mum, it might be someone nice like the vanhootins or your cristians?" But mum didn't say anything, she just shook her head. I stood up, the buzzer for the door was on the wall just there, I said "shouldn't we find out who it is, because if its someone nice then we can ask them to bring us some more food" but mum put her hand over the buzer, she said "if its him and we answer then he'll know we're up here."

I thought "all right" so I sat down again, I thought "we won't do anything then." I looked at mum's drawing of the fort and I said "so where will the enemy go?" Mum sat down too, and that was when we heard it. The front door was behind us, you see, so you could hear right through it, and suddenly there was a noise, it was quite small, it went "tap tap tap" and it was footsteps. I looked at mum and her eyes went wide, I said "its probably just someone going to another flat" because there were lots in the building you see, but then the footsteps kept getting louder and louder. Then mum got up, she ran into the kitchen and she came back with a nife, it wasn't like the tiny ones in my bed it was a big one, you would cut up something big like a chicken with it, and she whispered, and though her voice was quiet it was like she was shouting, that was funny, it was like she was spitting it, she said "I'm not going to let him hurt you." I thought "what will I do?" I looked at the door and the lock was locked, the key was in it, the bolt was shut too, so I thought "that's all right" but then I turned round and picked up a chair anyway, I picked it up so I could hit him on his head.

I was all ready when the footsteps stopped, I thought "he is just outside" that was strange, I thought "hes just inches away" I thought "if it wasn't for this door I could just reach out and touch him, I could hit him with my chair." Then suddenly there was the knock on the door, it sounded so loud, it was like it was a gun, and a voice said "Hannah, are you there?" and I thought "wait a minute" I thought "its not dad after all" and just for a moment I thought "its all right, its Franseen" and I wanted to just open the door. But then I looked at mum and she was frowning and holding her nife so I thought "oh no you don't Franseen you traiter cat" and I gave mum a special angry look, I held my chair a bit higher and mum gave me a little serious nod, so it was nice actually, it was like we were solders in a battile.

Then something funny happened, there was another voice and it said "Hannah, Lawrence, Jemima, are you there, we tried your doorbell but I'm not sure its working." I could hardly believe it actually, but this time I was readier, I didn't think "oh hurrah" I thought "Crissy chick, you too" I thought "how dare you after all I did, trying to cheer you up passing the salt and telling you about our amusement park." I was so angry, I thought "he has turned them all against us" I thought "she was our freind, I really hate you, dad."

Then I got worried, I thought "what if Jemima wakes up because they are shouting, she won't understand, she will run out and shout hello and they'll know we're in here." So I gave mum a look to say "I have to do something" I put my chair down really carefully so it didn't make any scrapeing noise, and I went back to our bedroom, I closed the door with just a tiny click, and it worked, she didn't wake up at all. When I got back mum was pointing at the floor and I saw a piece of paper got pushed under the door, I could see writing on it and it said "we came over but you were out, think your phone isn't working, give us a ring, love Franseen and Crissy."

Then I heard their footsteps again and this time they were going away down the stairs, so I thought "oh good, hurrah" and that was when I noticed. I listened really carefully and suddenly I thought "why didn't I notice that before" and I felt all shivery. Even though they were quite far away now I was careful, I told mum in a wisper "listen to the footsteps, dyou hear?" She gave me a look like she was saying "what d'you mean" so I said "there aren't two lots, there are three. He's down there." Mum gave me a look like she was really surprised, but then she listened really carefully and then she whispered back "oh god, Lawrence, your right."

WE ARE IN A GALAXY called the Milky Way, you can see it if it isn't cloudy, it looks like a big blur in the sky. The Milky Way is huge, it is shaped like a flying soucer with arms going round and round, and we are half way to the edge.

One day scientists decided they really wanted to know whats right in the middle of the Milky way, they thought "I bet theres something really intresting." They looked through their telescopes and they saw there was a big bulge which was really crowded, there were so many stars that if earth was there there wouldn't ever be night, it would be day all the time because lots of suns would wizz around the sky in different directions, I think it would be really hard to sleep. Scientists noticed the bulge is like a real battlefield, there are huge huge stars which don't last long, suddenly they just blow up, so the bulge is full of broken bits of them.

Then scientists said "wait a minute, we still don't know whats right in the middle of the Milky way. Whats in the middle of that bulge?" It was hard to see because all the blown up bits of stars got in the way, but the scientists kept trying, they used all their teliscopes, and eventually they noticed a little tiny star that was really near the middle, it was going round and round it very fast. The scientists thought "thats intresting." So they watched the star really carefully, they knew it was going round something, and though they couldn't see this something because it was all dark, they could find out lots about it anyway, just from the way the star wizzed round it. They said "lets see, this something is quite small but it is really really heavy, it is millions of times heavier than the sun, and its dark so we can't see it at all." Then suddenley they said "wait a minute, actually we know just what this is, oh no, this is a disaster, how horrible, its a big black hole."

Now the scientists got really worried, they thought "what if that black hole just gets bigger and bigger, what if it swallows up everything, eventually it will swallow up the whole galaxy, it will swallow up earth and everyone will get killed." But then they looked at it more carefully and they weren't sure. They said "perhaps its not so bad actually, it doesnt look like it is swallowing up much right now, everything just keeps going round and round." So they decided "actually perhaps its useful, perhaps it keeps the galaxy from just flying apart, otherwise the stars would wizz off all over the place." So they changed their mind, they said "dyou know perhaps this black hole is really our friend."

I thought "this flat is much better than the cottage was, its so high up that dad can't ever get in through the windows, he would have to have special sticky feet like spiderman." Those days were good actually. Mum wasn't cross or sad or scraching any more, and I did lots of things to help her, I had really good ideas. I closed all the shutters opposite dads building, I thought "now you can't see us after all, dad, so you will feel really silly." I told Jemima "we have to keep them closed or it will get too hot."

Jemima was the worst trouble, because she was too young to undestand. She kept saying "I want to go out, I want to have an ice cream, I want to go on the swings" she said "I'm bored of eating spaggetties with red sauce, I want to go out and have pizza" and when we said "no you can't Jemima, not today" she just shreeked. Even telling her she would get bitten by dogs only worked for a little while, then she said "I don't care, I'll hit the dogs with a stick." I tried to help, I read to her from my tintins and I even let her play with my hot wheels. Mum had a good idea too, she said "I know its borring, lamikin, but if your good then when the dogs have gone away and we can go out again you can have your own hamster." Jemima was really pleased, she said "oh yes, I'll be good" but even that didn't last very long, soon she started saying "when can I go out and get my hamster?" But I thought "actually it doesn't really matter" because even though it was anoying when she screemed she couldn't do anything really, because mum hid the key to the door on a high shelf she couldn't reach, so she couldn't get out.

Once a funny thing happened. It was the afternoon and I looked through the shutters at dads building and there was a big surprise, because there in the window was an old lady, she was watering a plant. I thought "wait a minute, who are you?" so I went to find mum, I had to be careful because Jemima was with her so I said "mum, I'm spelling a word, can you come and help me" I thought "that will work" because Jemima can't write anything yet, and it did, she didn't follow mum, she just sat there watching telly in Italian. I whispered "look mum, theres a funny old lady in dads building." Mum looked but then she just shook her head, she wispered "it must just be the cleener." I saw her again once actually, it was in the night and she was walking past a window, so I thought "you are lazy dad, why don't you clean your flat like we do?"

We did my new fort, and it was really good this time. Mum cut the walls and battelments with one of the little sharp nives that dad put in our beds, and I did lots of the staples, we painted it with the creem paint, it had a draw bridge with real string and the floors of the towers weren't wobbly now so I put the enemy up there, he didn't fall over, and I did lots of battles, I let Jemima fire the catupult. Sometimes the doorbell rang, it wasn't very often and nobody ever came up the stairs again, that was good, but it was annoying, actually, because we couldn't see who was down there, because if we looked out of the window then they would see us of course, they would know we were there.

Then I had a clever idea, and when it was really late again I did it with mum. First I got the screw driver and I unscrewed a mirror from the bathroom, it was quite small and round and it had a long strechy arm like a trelis, mum said it was a shaving mirror. Then we fixed one of the shutters with wire so it was just open a little bit, and we fixed the mirror to it with more wire, we did it so you could see who was standing by the door downstairs, and after that I always ran and looked to see who it was. Every day really early in the morning it rang but I was never quick enough and they were already gone, mum said it was just garbagemen. Later when we were getting up and having breakfast it rang again, that was the postman, I saw him. Once it was Franseen, that was a bit scary, but she didnt come up the stairs this time, I thought "oh good, its locked" I think she put something in the post box but that didn't matter. And once mums cristians came, they rang the bell four times really loudly like they were cross, so we told Jemima it wasn't for us, somebody was just playing a stupid joke.

The best time was in the night when Jemima was asleep and me and mum stayed up, so it was just like the old days. We guarded the flat, we watched television, which was so we could improove our italian, and sometimes we made pop corn, mum found two bags in a cubord. Once it was funny, it was really really late, I think it was almost dawn, when mum suddenly said "let's have some choclate" which was bad actually because there wasn't that much left, we were supposed to share it with Jemima, but instead we just ate a whole bar. Then mum did a really funny thing, she did a kind of dance in front of the windows, our shutters were shut of course, she pointed towards dads building and she shouted "ha ha ha ha" it was like she was saying "you can't get us" and then I did it too, that was really good, we ran up and down and we gigelled.

The next night something bad happened. Mum went out of the sitting room for a bit, I hardly notised actually, I was watching the telly, it was about a train, when suddenly she came back and I knew something went wrong because her face was all worried. All she said was "Lawrence" but it was funny, we hardly needed to say anything any more, it was like I knew anyway. So I followed her into the kitchen, she showed me a soucepan on the cooker and I could see what was strange right away, I thought "I am getting clever like mum now, I just know everything." So I just pointed and said "that?" and I was right, mum noded. You see in the water there was some white stuff, it was really thin and

171

sort of floating, it was like wisps. Mum said "I just boiled it earlier, I was going to make some tea but then I changed my mind,
thank god." She said "smell it" and it didn't smell of anything
much, actually, it was like metal. I said "so it came from the taps"
I thought "uhoh that's bad" and mum said "Beppo must have
shown him where the pipe is." I thought "I never liked that
Beppo with his stupid car with no floor" I thought "thank goodness mum didn't drink that tea."

Mum started getting upset, I knew she would, she said "I
don't know what we'll do now, we've got nothing to drink, we
can't have baths, we can't even wash our hands, because the poisson will go straight through our skin." Then she gave me a look
and she said "I just don't see how we can stay here any longer,
Lawrence love." But I thought "there must be some way" so I said
"we can't just let him chase us out" I said "don't worry mum,
we'll think of something." Jemima really likes her baths, so we
found the pipe where all the water came in, we had to look for it
all over the place but we found it in the end, it was in the bathroom, and we switched it off. When Jemima woke up mum said
"I'm afraid the water doesn't work any more, lamikin, so you can't
have your bath today" and then she switched on a tap to show it
didn't work, it just made a funny noise like it was breatheing,
and though Jemima still shouted "but I want my bath, I want it"
there was nothing she could do.

I checked everywhere and there were only two bottles of water and one was fizzy which me and Jemima don't like, it goes up
your nose. I thought "they won't last long." I tried to read a
Tintin, red sea sharks, but it was hard because I kept stopping

and thinking "there must be something we can do" so I forgot which picture I was on, I thought "I must think of a plan." First I thought "what if we get water from someone elses pipe instead?" but then we would have to make a big hole in the wall, and I knew we would never manage that, actually, it would be impossible. Then I thought "what about the rain" I thought "we can get it from the guter" but when I looked out of the window I saw the guter was really high so we couldn't reach, and anyway there wasn't any rain, it was a lovely sunny day. After that I thought "what if we got someone to send us some bottles of minerel water" but then I thought "but who?" and that was impossible too, because dad had probably turned them all against us now, so even if they sent us minerel water it would just be poissoned. So in the end all I did was pour the fizzy water into a big bowl and stir it a bit to make the bubbles go away.

Suddenly mum was shaking my arm to make me wake up, so I thought "uhoh I fell asleep again" I thought "what has he done now" but I was wrong, because then I noticed mum was smiling like I hadn't seen for days, that was a surprise, that was good, that was wonderful, I thought "whats happened now?" Jemima was awake, she was playing with her animals, so we had to be careful, mum took me to the window, she pointed with her finger towards dads building and she whispered "he's gone away." So I looked quickly and all of dads shutters were shut again now. I whispered back "are you sure mum? He's not just pretending?" and she said "I'm quite sure, he's gone back to Scotland again on rionair, can't you feel it? Look, the yellow cars gone too." And d'you know I could feel it, that was wonderfull, it was like the air was different now, it was all sort of empty and nice now that dad was gone away. I wispered "hurrah" and d'you know Jemima was smiling, I thought "she can feel it too, even though she doesn't know anything."

So we did something amazing. We undid the bolt and unlocked the lock and then we just walked right out of the flat. I looked up at dads building with its shut shutters and I stuck out my tongue, I thought "ha." It felt funny walking down a road after being inside for so long, it was so good, I watched a tram go past and I thought "look at that, isnt it noisy" and when Jemima got worried and said "what about the dogs" mum and me both laughed, I said "don't worry Jemima, they all went home." First we went to the roasticheria and had riceballs, it was a snack just for fun, they were really delicious and hot. Then we went to the supermarket, we got some more food, mostly it was biscuits and things, actually, and we got some more mineral water, mum got Jemima some sweets and she got me a bit of parmer ham, which I really like but she said I couldn't have last time because it was too expensive, she said it was my treat because I was such a good boy.

When we got back I wispered to mum "what about the taps, dyou think he's stopped doing the water now?" and mum said "we'll have to see." So she got Jemima to play with her dolls and we went secretly and switched on the main tap from the pipe. Mum ran the water for a long time, then she filled up a glass and looked at it really carefully, she smelt it too, and suddenly she smiled, she said "its fine." I thought "oh hurrah" I went and told Jemima "you can have your bath now, the waters working again" and Jemima said "oh yes" so it was like we were having a party. We had our lunch, mum said we must or it would already be suppertime, and I had my parma ham, it was really delicious.

After I thought "everything is so good, it is like we are all back to normal, perhaps mum can go back to her job with her cristians, perhaps we can go back to the vanhootins, that would be nice" but then I thought "but we must still be careful just in case" so I made a new plan. I went all round the flat but there weren't many bottles actually, there were five empty minerel water bottles and two big glass bottles with little handles. I thought "this isn't enough, we need hundreds" but I filled them up anyway, then I put them in a neat line by the beeday in the bathroom, I had to roll the glass ones along the floor because they were so heavy, I thought "its a start."

I wanted to go and get some more at once, just in case dad came back really suddenly, so I thought "I will go and ask mum where we can get them." But then a strange thing happened, because I couldn't find her anywhere. I looked in the kitchen and the sitting room and in her bedroom but it was like she had just vanished. I thought "thats funny" I thought "she's always here, she can't have just gone off." I didn't like it actually, I thought "I hope she didn't just go away when I was doing the bottles" and I felt all shivery, I could feel my breatheing going fast. Everything was so quiet, Jemima was sleeping again, so I went to wake her up, because suddenly I wanted her to come and look with me, but then I didn't after all because I had a new idea, I thought "what if shes on the balcony?" We hardly went there, you see, because mum said we mustn't, she said she didn't like the look of the railing, though there was a nice view, you could see a doame. I went towards the kitchen where the doors to the balcony were, and it was funny, it was like I didn't want to look just in case she wasn't there after all, I thought "what will I do then?"

But she was there, she had taken a chair out and she was sitting in the sun. I thought "oh good" but it didn't last, because then I notised she looked all sad. Mum changed so quickly, one moment she was all fine and then it was like a big ray just shon on her and made her go wrong. I thought "not again" and I was annoyed, actually, I thought "you were all right just now, why can't you just stay chearful?" I said "hello mum" but she didn't even look at me, she didn't say hello, she just said in her yawn voice, it was like a weeze "I can't fight him any more, Lawrence. He'll be back again soon, I know it, he'll just get another rionair."

I thought "I will tell her my plan, that will make her better" so I did, I said "even if he comes back he won't be able to get us this time because we'll have all our water, so it won't matter if he does the pipe, I've already done seven bottles." But it didn't work at all, she waved her hand like she was angry, it was like I made her get a headacke, she said "for gods sake, Lawrence, wake up. Can't you see, we'll never be safe, he'll get us if he wants to. We can't stop him with any plan, he'll poison the air or break down the door, he'll find a way."

I sat down on the balcony and suddenly I felt really tired. I looked at the doame and I noticed it had scaffolding on it so I thought "that's all broken." I said "what should we do then?" but mum didn't answeer, it was like her batteries all got used up when she was cross at me just now, there wasn't anything left. I looked at her but she wasn't moving at all, she just sat really still on her chair with her arms squashing her sides like she wanted to be a bird, it was like she was cold. I thought "what will I do now" and I didn't know, there wasn't anything. So I just sat there, it went on for ages, I listened to cars going in the road, sometimes there was a tram, and I felt a bit cold too, there was a breeze. I thought "my plans never work, I cannot help mum at all, I cannot make us safe." I thought "mum thinks my bottles of water are just a stupid waste of time." I thought "its funny, its like we were walking on a lovely hill and then suddenly we are right on the cliff and theres no way back, we are stuck forever." I thought "I can't even do more bottles without mum, because I can't just go out and do it by myself, I don't know where you get hundreds of empty bottles, I can't speak italian."

Suddenly I got so cross, I thought "everythings spoiled now." And that's when I said that thing. It wasn't serius actually, I didn't really mean it. I said "maybe we should just . . ." and it was like a joke, you see, my "maybe we should just . . ." It was a joke about how we could stop dad from coming and getting us after all.

Mum didn't say anything. I thought "she doesn't like anything I say anymore, she doesn't even like my jokes" but then I notised something. You see, though she was still just sitting still in her chair with her arms like a bird, her eyes weren't just switched off anymore, it was like they were going awake now, they were thinking. Then she turned her head round really slowly and she looked at me, she said "you know, Lawrence, perhaps your right, perhaps we should."

CHAPTER SIX

One day Emporer Nero had some really bad news, because there was a rebellion against him in France, which was called gaul then. Nero thought "oh no this is terrible, what will I do?" Sometimes there was good news so it looked like everything might be all right after all, so Nero had a big dinner with lots of delicious food, he asked his friends. When it was bad news again he made up rude songs about all his enimies.

After a while he thought "I really must make a plan." First he thought "I know, I will execute all my generels so they can't become enemies too." But then he thought "no, I will execute all the gauls instead, that will serve them right." Then he changed his mind again, he was always doing it, actually, and he thought "I know, I will tell my solders that if they defeat all my enemies they can steal everything in Gaul, that will work. No no, wait a minute, I will execute all the senaters, that is a better plan, I will invite them to a big dinner and poisson them all at once." Finally he thought "I know, I will burn rome down again, but I will do it much better this time, I will get thousands of wild animals and let them all go so when people run out into the road because their houses are on fire they will get eaten."

But after that he changed his mind all over again, he decided to get a big army and go and fight. It took ages, he needed hundreds of carts to carry all his theater scenery in case he wanted to sing, and he needed lots of money so he could pay his soldiers, but nobody gave him any because they didn't like him. So he made a new plan, he said "I know, when the battle is going to start I will walk up to the enemy army all by myself, I won't take my sword or anything, and suddenly I will just weep and weep. When the enemy solders see me they will be so surprised that they will stop fighting, they will all start weeping too, they will shout 'oh Nero we are so sorry we attacked you' and then they will execute all their generels, so I will win."

But in the end he didn't do that plan either, he just stayed at home and waited. When he was sleeping he had terreble dreams about all the people he executed and the worst ones were about his mother Agripina, she shouted "how dare you Nero, I really hate you for putting me in the collapsible boat, I really hate you for executing me like that." He bought a big box of poisson to drink when his enimies came.

Then one day he woke up in the night, I think he wanted a glass of water or something, so he called out for his servants, but nothing happened. He thought "that's strange." So he got up and walked round his palace which was huge, it was his golden house, he shouted "hello, where are you" but nobody ansewered, because there was nobody there you see, it was empty and all the rooms were locked. Suddenly Nero noticed that everything was stolen, all the tables and chairs and the sheets on the beds were gone, and so was his box of poisson, so he thought "uhoh, what will I do, I can't kill myself after all." He rushed out of the palace to try and find a gladiator to stab him but the gladiators had run away too. Then he thought "all right, I will just jump in the river Tibber" but then he changed his mind again, he saw three of his servants and they said "lets go to our house in the country, Nero, its really near."

They went on horses, Nero didn't have any shoes or socks because he got up so quickly that he hadn't got dressed properly. He hid his face in his hat so nobody would recognize him, because everybody was going round saying "I wonder where Nero is, the enemy army is coming." When he got to the servants house he was really hungary and thirsty because he hadn't had his breakfast, but there was nothing there, so even though he was emporer he had to eat old bread and drink water out of a nasty pond.

Nero thought "this is terreble, I don't want to die, I am such a wonderful singer, I want to sing lots more songs." But then he saw some enemy solders riding on their horses and his servants said "watch out they will put you in a wooden fork and hit you with metal sticks until you are dead." So Nero said "oh no, that sounds horreble" and he quickly stabed himself with his sword and died. That was the end of Emporer nero.

But there was a strange thing. Nero was dreadful, nobody liked him because he executed thousands of Romans and took all their money, he spent it all on his delicious dinners and his golden House, he was a terrible singer and he cheated in all the compititions. But after he was dead some people weren't sure after all, they said "poor old Nero." It was like they forgot everything and they didn't know any more, they got confused, so they thought "yes he was strange but he was our emporer. Its a shame hes gone now, we miss him, actually, we feel really sad." They put flowers on his graive and they cried. They even made little statues of him and put them in special places. So it was almost like he was a god after all.

Mum said I didn't need to pack much because we would be back soon, she said I could only have one bag, so it should have been really easy, but I kept on changing my mind. I thought "I will take all my tintins" but then I thought "reading tintins makes me get car sick, I will take my lego so I can play that in the car." Mum wasn't sad at all any more, she was serious, she was talking and talking about our new plan, she was whispering so Jemima wouldn't wake up, because it was the middle of the night again, you see. It was like my idea about "how to stop dad from getting us after all" was a big empty room and she was filling it up with chairs and tables and things, because as she talked and talked it got full of little plans, so it was more real.

Sometimes I wasn't sure actually, I thought "it was just a joke really" I thought "I wonder if she will change her mind, she might" but then I got angry again, it was like a big engine started wirring. I thought "but he is horrible though, spying on us like that from his building and putting nives in my bed and poisson in the water and the strawberry cake and turning all mums freinds against us." I thought "mum says it will just take a few days and then we can come back and live in our flat again, and we will be safe, that will be lovely."

Then I was in my bed again and mum was leaning over me and saying "Lawrence love, wake up" so I must have fallen asleep. It was just getting light, when I looked out of the gap in the shutter the sky was half blue and half orange and I felt so tired I could hardly keep my eyes open, it was like they were glude. Mum had black lines under her eyes, I thought "she is like a leemer" and she said "I'm really sorry, I know its early, but its better if we get a good start." Jemima was so cross getting woken up that she shrieked, but she was better when we told her we were going back to the cottage to get more toys, which was a lie of course, she said "oh yes, I want all my animals, and all my dolls too, I want everything."

When we had our breakfast I felt a bit better, and I was just going to pee when I noticed something. When I looked out of the window, I saw that the shutters on dads bulding were all open again. That was a surprise, I thought "does that mean he didn't go after all, did he come straight back again on rionair?" I thought "uhoh, what will we do now?" So I went back to the kitchen and I said "mum can you help me with my bag" which was so Jemima wouldn't realize, and it worked, because Jemima was so busy eating her toast that she didn't even look up. When I showed dads shutters to mum she sort of blinked, but then she just shook her head and she said "its nothing, Lawrence. It'll just be the cleaner" so I thought "all right then, mum" I thought "that's good I think."

Mums bags were already packed, she just had two, and she packed Jemimas for her, so we were all ready to go when something dreadfull happened. Mum put all the bags by the door but then she turned round and she said "I almost forgot, we'd better leave lots of water and food for Hermann." I didn't undestand, I said "what d'you mean mum" I thought "does she want everything to be ready for him when we come back?" So I said "we don't need to do that now, mum, it'll just get old if we leave it out." But mum made a face like she was thinking "don't be silly, Lawrence," and she said "he'll be fine if we leave lots" she said "we can't take him with us, Lawrence, you must see that, he hasn't got a pets passport remember, what if they stop us?" I couldn't believe it, I thought "how can you mum, this is Hermann remember" I said "but we can't just leave him all by himself, he'll die." Mum didn't even say sorry, she just looked like she was really tired and she said "I suppose we could ask somebody in the building to look after him" but that was just as bad of course, because dad had turned them all against us too, they would put poisson wisps in his water.

Suddenley I was so cross, it was like I really hated mum, it was like I wanted to shout so loud she would break into little bits, she would just go away. I gave her my worst look, and I said "I'm not coming without Hermann, you'll just have to go by yourself" and Jemima started too, because she really likes Hermann of course, she said "we can't leave him behind." So mum gave up, she put her hands in the air like she was really annoyed and she said "this is so stupid." I didn't say anything, I just took Hermann in his cage down the stairs myself, I put him beside me in the car and I said "its all right now Hermann, your coming." Even then I was still cross with mum for ages, I thought "I cant believe she said that."

It was strange being in the car on the motor way again, Mum and me and Hermann and Jemima, so it was just like when we came, which seemed like years ago now. I looked at Hermann, he was sleeping in his nest but I could see the end of his nose sticking out of the straw, and I looked out of the window at the country side, there were tiny little towns right on top of mountains, I thought "I am just fine now, actually, I am quite all right." I thought "we are like a secret army now, nobody in these cars knows what we are doing" I thought "we are like the Colonnas when they went across Italy to get pope Bonniface" I thought "we are like Secret Eagles going on our way."

But I did get annoyed because we were going so slowly. I watched all the signs you see, they were for Bologna or Milano, which is Milan, or Firenze, which means Florence, but they were so slow it was like they hardly changed at all. I thought "we've been going for hours but it still says Firenze 119 and Florence is really near Rome, we will never get to Scotland like this, it will take months." I thought "what if he goes away again before we get there, what if he comes back with rionair." Suddenly it was like I was all ichy, I wanted to go really fast so everything would just be done, it would be all finished. I said "hurry up mum, can't you go faster?" but she said "Lawrence I told you I'm going as fast as I can, we don't want to get stopped for speeding." Then Jemima made it worse like she always does, it was like she wanted to stop us ever getting there, she said "mummy I have to pee" or "mummy I want some pizza" so we went to service stations twice, which was really annoying. When she said "I want to pee" again I said "you can't, Jemima, all right, you'll just have to do a pee in your pants" and that made mum cross, she said "Lawrence for goodness sake" but I didn't care, I thought "I won't let us stop again, I will shout and shout and make us go faster."

Then all at once we were at a service station, mum was driving into a parking place so I thought "oh no not again." I said "mum we have to keep going, we have to get to Florence" but mum just laughed, she said "you've been asleep for hours, Lawrence love, we're miles past Florence now, in fact we're past Bologna." That made me feel a bit better, so I didn't mind when we stopped. And actually we didn't take long, because we just got more petrol, mum said "god that's a lot, I'm sure its gone up since we drove down here" and Jemima got cross, she said "I want pizza" but mum said we had lots of biscuits to eat in the car, and I helped her, I said "that's much better, Jemima, because then we'll get your toys even sooner."

After that it was the boring bit, its just flat and nothing to see except motorway and cars and buildings, sometimes we got stuck in traffic jams, so I started playing a new game. I told Jemima "d'you know we're not really on the motorway at all. That view out of the window isn't real you see, its like a computer screene, really we are parked on that hill with a lovely view of rome." Jemima thought this was really funny, she said "actually we are outside Crissies house" and I said "no, we are in the car park at Ikeyer." Then I thought "I know I will make this more intresting" so I said "actually we are in space, we are going towards a big black hole" and Jemima said "oh yes, look there is a shooting star." After that I said "no no, we are in the sea" and I really liked that one, I said "uhoh, we are sinking, we are going deeper and deeper, the water is really cold, watch out Jemima that giant squid is going to break all the windows with his tentecles, then the car will start filling up with water and it will get higher and higher till we can't breath." But Jemima didn't like the game any more, she started crying so mum said "stop it Lawrence. Can't you see your upsetting her."

Then a strange thing happened. Everything was quiet, we were just driving across more flat italy, a sign said "milano 72" and suddenly I felt really sad that I made Jemima cry, it was like this was the worst thing I ever did, which was silly, actually, because usually I don't mind, because its her fault anyway. I thought "I wish I had something to give her, I wish I had a little sweet" I thought "I would let her play with my lego but I forgot to put it in the car, its in the boot" and it was almost like I wanted to cry because I couldn't let her play with my lego, that was funny. I thought "I will tell her we won't ever go to the bottom of the sea again, that will be something" but then when I looked she was in dreemland again, her head was falling over the edge of her car seat, so I didn't say anything.

Later I looked out of the window and we were going past the fair ground where we went before. I saw the big wheel and I thought "it was nice going there" and I wondered if mum would stop again, though I knew we mustn't because we were in a big hurry, I thought "perhaps she will" but she just went right past. Then I decided "I've got an idea, I will remember everything we

did there, all the machines we went on and mum speaking italian and what we all said" mum always says I have an amazing
memory. I thought "if I remember it all then it will take just as
long as when we were there, it will be like we are doing it all
again" and I really tried, I thought and thought, but it was hard,
I kept thinking of other things instead, they just pushed in, so I
had to start all over again, I couldn't help it.

When Jemima woke up she said "I'm bored of these biscuits,
I want pizza, I want chicken, I want sweets" but mum said "we
can't stop driving now, lamikin" that was good. We drove and
drove until it got dark, I could see all the other cars head lights,
and I thought "it feels like I've been in this car forever, I can't believe we just started this morning." Then I must have fallen asleep
again because I woke up and we weren't driving any more, we
were parked in a little road by some trees, it was in the country
side. It was a bit cold in the car, but mum had put my jacket on
me like a blankit, I thought "that's nice" and though I had some
ackes from sitting in the car for so long I didn't mind actually, I
thought "if we went to a hotel it would have taken ages and
wasted all of mums money, so this is better." I couldn't sleep, I
could hear mum and Jemima breathing. I was hungry so I ate
some more biscuits though I was really fed up with them now, I
drank some fanta but it was warm and there were hardly any bubbles. I thought "these biscuits are really loud when I crunch
them" I thought "I wonder if mum and Jemima will wake up?"
but they didn't, Jemima just started snoring. So I looked up out
of the window at the sky and I thought "where are you black hole
in the bulge in the middle of the Milky way?" I thought "where

are you Great Attractor?" but it was a bit cloudy, I could just see a few stars, they looked really small.

When I woke up it was morning, we were driving on the motor way and Jemima was saying "I want a crusson and some apple juice" but mum said "we haven't got time just now lamikin, maybe we'll stop and have some later." So we drove and drove, until I notised a sign that said "Paris 82" and then mum turned round and wispered to me, because Jemima was in dreamland again, she said "we're doing so well, d'you know we might even get to Scotland tonight." I thought "oh this is new" I thought "wow, it didn't take months at all" and it was funny, suddenly I felt really strange, it was like I wanted to go faster and slower all at the same time, I didn't know which, it was like I wanted to get there right now this second, it was like we were late, but it was like I never wanted to get there at all. Then I must have fallen asleep again, because when I woke up there was a sign for England, mum said that's what it was, it said Angletaire and suddenly I felt so exited, even though we were only going back for a day or two to stop dad getting us after all I thought "hurrah hurrah, we are going home."

The numbers on the signs for the channell tunnell got smaller and smaller, and though it was silly because I knew we couldn't, I kept thinking "wouldn't it be nice to see all my friends, Tommy and Ritchie and Peter Norris, I wonder what kittens Tania Hodgsons cat had, were they all tabies, I wonder what Mr Simmons taught everyone at school?" Suddenly we were really near the tunnell, I saw the sea behind a wall, Jemima was shouting "on a train, on a train" and that was when I remembered. I thought "oh no, this is a disaster, how did I forget, thats so stupid" and I said "wait mum, what about Hermann?" because he was in his cage right beside me, anybody could just look in and see.

Mum said "oh god" and she made the car swerve a bit so we stopped by the side of the road so the other cars could go past. I said "should I hide him in my pockit?" though I wasn't sure actually, Phil Greene brought his mouse to school in his pocket once and it escaped and got lost, they never found it. Mum said "let's put his cage in the boot." So that's what we did, I folded up a piece of paper and stuck it in the side of the wheel so it wouldn't go round and make a squeak, poor Hermann tried to make it work and he gave me a sad look, I said "sorry Hermann." Then we covered his cage with a blankit and Jemima said "what will they do if they find him, will they put him in jail" so I got annoyed, I said "shut up Jemima, its none of your busness." When we got back into the car and drove off again mum said "I didn't even look to see if there was a camera, oh god" she told us that when we showed our passports to the passport man we must smile but not too much, we must just look really normal.

I tried to practice looking normal, I looked at my face in the window but it was hard to see, actually, with all the cars and road and sky behind, I looked seethrough like a goast, so I couldn't tell if I was normal or not, and then mum parked at the place where we got our tickets. She said "I hope we don't have to wait too long for a train, sometimes they're full" so I thought "what about poor Hermann, if it takes ages he might sufocaite under that blanket" I wanted to get him out again but mum said "Lawrence, just leave him."

Then she locked us in and we just sat there, Jemima hummed itsy bitsy spider and kicked the chair in front like she does, and I tried not to think about Hermann, I thought "oh look theres a plane really high up, its like a piece of chalk thats drawing a line all by itself." I thought "mums being a really long time getting our tickets." Finally she came back out but her face looked all worrid so I knew something went wrong, and I was right, actually, when she got in the car she said "I just don't believe this, none of my credit cards worked, I could have swarn there was just enough."

This was new, this was bad. I said "what will we do?" and Jemima said "but I want to go now, I want my animals and my dolls" then mum said "quiet you two, I'm trying to think." She was scraching herself, the back of her hand was all red, and she said "we'll just have to sell something I suppose, but what, all I can think of is the car" but me and Jemima both shouted "no no." I said "you can't mum, its ours, its like our house, and then we'll just be stuck here." Mum said "we could always take a train" but I said "what about all our things, they're really heavy, how will we carry them" and mum said "I suppose I could sell my rings."

So we turned round and drove into a town, mum said "god we're almost out of petrol too and I've only got ten yuros left." We went to some shops and mum talked in French but it wasn't as good as her italian, she kept starting and stopping like it needed new batteries. Mum got cross, she said "they're worth twice that, I suppose they can see I'm desperate." That made me sad actually, I thought "poor mums rings" I thought "I really like them, especially the one with the pretty red bit" so I said "are you really sure you have to sell them" but mum said "I'm afraid so, Lawrence." So we went back to the first shop and the man gave her some yuros, mum said "that'll do for now."

Everything was taking longer and longer, I was so annoyed I just wanted to kick something. Jemima said "I'm hungary, I want a sandwich" and when I said "you can't Jemima" mum said "I think we all need some lunch." It took ages, Jemima is such a slow eater, its like she does it on purpose, and then she screamed so everybody looked round until mum got her rasberry ice cream. I thought "now, at last" but then we found we couldn't go on the next train after all because it was full, we had to wait for the third. I wispered to mum "does that mean we can't go to Scotland to-day after all?" and she said "I'm afraid not Lawrence" so I got even crosser, I thought "its all Jemimas fault, we should have just left her in rome in the flat with lots of water and bread."

But then something good happened, that was a surprise. We drove off the train in England and I thought "now we will go on the motorway again" but we didn't actually, instead mum went onto a little road and stopped in a car park by a supermarket. She turned round in her seat to look at me and she said "haven't you forgotten something?" I didn't know, I said "what d'you mean?" and she laughed, she said "Hermann of course." I said "oh yes, hurrah hurrah," that was wonderfull, because you see nobody noticed him after all, so they wouldn't put him in jail. We got him out of the boot and he was fine, he wasn't suffocated, so I took out the piece of paper and he went round and round in his wheel, I gave him new water and nuts and he gave me a look like he was saying "thank you Lawrence."

THE BLACK HOLE IN THE MIDDLE of the Milky way is quite small but its still terrible, its greedy like a big mouth and once anything goes in it never comes back out again, it is gone forever. There is a secrit line all round it, nobody can see it but it is there, its called the Event Horizon, and you must be really careful, you mustn't ever go across it by accident or you will get sucked into the black hole right away, nothing can stop you and you will never come out again.

There is lots of dust by the event horizon, its like a big disk, it goes round faster and faster until it falls in, so it is like water going down the plug hole. And d'you know just because its about to fall down the dust does a funny thing, it spits out lots of rays, they are X rays and radio waves, scientists can see them through their teliscopes, and they are awful actually. It is like the poor dust is screeming, its saying "oh no I'm getting sucked into this black hole, I will never come back, nobody will ever see me again, I will get squoshed flat, this is terrible" its like it is saying "help me."

It was getting dark and Jemima was shouting "oh look there's the church and there's the shop, theres mrs Potters house and the trees like funny hair, we're really almost there now" and I was thinking "uhoh, now there will be trouble, because I bet dad has got in and broken everything, what will we tell Jemima, will we say its burglars?" But actually he hadn't after all, that was a surprise, everything was just the same, so it was strange walking into the sitting room and seeing all our things still on the floor from our packing. When we sat down at the table and had our dinner, mum made beans on toast, I had a funny feeling, it was like we never went anywhere at all, we were just here all the time and rome wasn't real, it was like a film. But then I did a clever thing. I pulled out the Julius Cesaer, I had him in my pockit all the time you see, I said "there you are" and that made it real again.

The next morning it was funny waking up in my old bed in the cottage, I thought "this is nice." Jemima didn't want to leave, she said "its nicer here, the water never goes dirty so I can always have my bath." Actually I wanted to stay too, I thought "just a little bit, just till tommorow" but of course I knew we couldn't really. Mum looked really tired, her eyes were funny like head lights, so I helped her, I said "there won't be that dirty water ever again, Jemima, when we go back you will have your bath every day, I promise" and then I said "now what toys do you want to take?" That worked, she wanted them all, I had to get more and more boxes from the skulery to put them in, she wanted all her animals and dolls and even stupid things like her big spinning top that doesn't go round properley because the handle got bent, it doesn't do its tune, and all her pens though lots were dried up because she never puts the lids back on.

So we got ready. I put Jemimas things in the car and when she wasn't looking I took some of her stupid things out, because otherwise there wouldn't be any room left, and I put my things in instead, it was the box she made me leave behind before we went to Rome because she had to have her dolls house, with my hot wheels track and my computer consel, I thought, "that's fair."

Then just when we were getting in the car she cheated, she said "but I don't want to go, I want to stay here, I want to go another time." Mum looked all desperete, she shut her eyes and said "Jemima for gods sake" but I was ready, because I guessed she would do this, you see. I just grabbed her and then I pulled her jacket down really quickly so her arms were stuck, so when she tried to run away she just fell over, that was funny. Then mum and me got her in the car, we just picked her up and put her in, mum buckelled her up and we drove off, she said "I'm sorry about this lamikin, but we just have to go" and I said "I don't care if your screening, Jemima, I will just put my hands over my ears so I can't hear."

At lunchtime we stopped in a town where mum went to a shop and sold the man all her silver candel stick and cups and other metal things that we almost took to rome but didn't because the car was full. That was a shame too, I thought "we never used that candel stick actually, because mum said it was only for special occasions, and now we are getting rid of it for ever." I think mum noticed I was a bit sad, because she said "its worth it if it gets us back to Rome, Lawrence love."

Then Jemima was trouble, she said "we've been driving for hours and hours, wheres that river with the nice trees we go past, wheres the channell tunnell" so mum said "we're not going there till tomorrow, lamikin, first we're going somewhere else, because I need to do some shopping." That was a lie of course, and a funny thing happened, it was like Jemima sort of guessed, sometimes she is clever like that, she knows things even though nobody tells here, I don't know how. She gave mum a look and she said "what shopping?" Mum said "tea and that sort of thing, lamikin, you can't get nice tea in Rome" and I thought "uhoh, now Jemima will say we can just get that in a supermarket" but she didn't, she said "I don't want to go shopping, I want to go back to the cottege" so it was all right after all, and she fell asleep just after we went past the "welcome to Scotland" sign.

I looked out of the window at some mountains, I thought "now I am in Scotland" and it was funny, I thought "yesterday morning I was in France, and the morning before yesterday I was in Rome" but I could hardly believe it actually, it was like I was looking the wrong way down a teliscope. It was getting dark but we didn't stop for supper, mum got some sandwiches at the last service station so we just ate them, mine was chicken and bacon, and mum held hers with her hand on the steering wheel, she said Jemima could have hers when she woke up. I was thinking "I wish we had more crisps, that was a really small packit" when suddenly I looked up and saw something, it was a sign that said "Edinburugh 17." I could hardly believe it, I thought "thats quick, usually it takes hours and hours" and even though miles are bigger than kilomiters we would still be there really soon, so I thought "wait a minute, not yet, I'm not ready."

Actually, I think mum wasn't ready either because when I looked in the little mirror at her face I could see her eyes were going blink blink and her shoulder sort of twiched like she wanted to scratch herself all over, but of course she couldn't because she was driving. Her voice was going really fast, she said "dam dam, I should have got it earlier, but I didn't want to when Jemima was awake." I said "get what mum?" but she didn't answewer, she just said "I'll try here." It was a service station but then she did a strange thing, she drove in quite slowly and then instead of stopping she just drove out again. I said "why did you do that mum?" and she said "didn't you see, Lawrence, there were cameras." So I said "why can't they have cameras?" and mum frowned, she said "its not good if they take our picture, Lawrence love, they won't understand."

It was like I knew all that, actually, but it still was a surprise, it made me feel all shivery. I said "what will they do if they take our picture?" and mum said "they won't, Lawrence" but I wanted to know, I wanted to stop feeling shivery, so I said "tell me mum, what'll they do?" and mum did a little laugh but it sounded strange, I didn't like it. She said "I don't know, they'd probably try and put me in jail or something, but they won't" and she said "don't you worry, Lawrence love, everythings going to be fine." I thought "I wish we could just go home" but I didn't say anything, I just kept quiet, it was like if I kept quiet then nothing would happen. I thought "I will just sit really still and read my tintin" but it was hard because it was dark and the lamposts light kept moving round and round like they were a big torch that was swinging. Suddenly I thought of another question, I really wanted to know actually, and I was just going to ask it when mum slowed down again, she said "this'll do, perfect" because we went past another service station and a big shop which was like a supermarket for cars and bicycles. We went round the corner and parked and mum said "I want you to wait here and look after Jemima, Lawrence, I won't be long. I'm going to lock you in, all right?"

It was funny being all alone locked in the car in the dark in

Scotland all of a sudden. It was a bit cold, the wind made a noise on the window and I tried to read my tintin but I couldn't, because every time I looked at the picture of captain Haddock saying "bashi bazooks" I forgot why he said it again. I looked out of the window and there was a fat man walking down the road with a tiny little dog like a chiwawa, it kept stopping and smelling things so he pulled its leesh to make it go again. I thought "mums been gone for ages, what if there was a camara after all but she didn't see it because it was hidden, what if they already took her picture, what if they already put her in jail." Then I thought "I won't think that any more, I will just make it go away" but I couldn't, actually, it just kept coming back all by itself, I thought "because we are locked in, we will be stuck in here forever."

Then mum came round the corner, that was lovley, she was all lops sided from carrying the petrol can which was red, and in her other hand she had a plastic bag. She came up to my window and gave me a little tiny smile, that was nice, and then she put the petrol can in the boot, she had to move everything round because it was so full of Jemimas dolls and animals and pens that didn't work.

After that she drove off again and I started recognizing everything, all the shops and roads and houses, so I thought "that means we're here." Suddenly we were on dads street and mum parked the car just across from his house, his lights were on so I thought "he's in." I thought "is this it then?" and I felt shivery again, but it wasn't, actually, mum just sat there waiting, so I thought "she is checking." We sat there for ages, I could hear Jemima snoring and there were tiny bits of rain falling on the car,

I could see them on the windshield, they made a tiny noise like "tip tip tip" and then suddenly there he was, he was walking into the front room holding something. I only saw him for a moment and then he sat down, he disappeared, and it was strange, because I tried to get really angry but it didn't work, I just thought "there you are dad" I thought "you've got your dinner and now your eating it as you watch telly."

Mum started the car, so I thought "where are we going now, are we going away? Has she changed her mind after all?" but she hadn't, she just went round the corner and parked there, so I thought "oh of course, she just doesn't want our car to get noticed." I thought "this really is it then" and though we had been driving here for days I thought "theres no time left, where did it all go?" I thought "what will I do?" Mum was turning round to undo her seatbelt, but I stopped her, I thought "but I want to ask my question" it was the one I thought of earlier when mum saw the car supermarket. So I asked it, I said "if they take our picture will they send me and Jemima to jail too?"

Mum gave me a funny look, she said "don't be silly, your both much too young, now stop this, Lawrence love, nobodies going to jail." Then she gave me a little smile like she was saying "are you allright now?" But she didn't understand, actually, because you see I wanted us all to go to jail, because then we would all be together, it would be quite nice actually, it would be like when we stayed at the agro turismo. I thought "if they put her in jail and they won't let us come too, then where will we go?" and suddenly everything was dreadful. I thought "no no, this is a horreble disaster" I thought "I won't let her" so I said "no mum, stop" and I reeched out to grab her, but d'you know I forgot about my seat belt, which was silly, so all I did was touch her elboe with my fingers. Mum undid her seat belt so I thought "she's just going anyway, she's not even going to answewer me, that's not fair" but I was wrong, actually, instead she turned round and lent through the seats so her face was looking right at my eyes. She didn't look worried any more, it was like she was happy actually, she said "Lawrence, we've just driven all the way across Yurope to do this, remember. If we give up now then dad will come straight down again on rionair and this time we won't be able to stop him from doing something terreble, he'll poisson the water or the air or the food. I'm not going to let him hurt you."

I thought "I don't want her to go" but then I thought "mums clever, shes always right" and then I thought "its nice being in the car like this, why don't we just stay here." And in the end I never really did decide what I thought of course, because then something happened. I should have geussed it would, that was really stupid, but then mum didn't either, we were so busy talking that we just forgot. Someone said "what d'you mean dad'll do something terreble?" and that someone was Jemima, because we woke her up, you see. I thought "uhoh, we forgot to wisper." I thought "this is bad, what'll we do now?" Then I thought "I know, I'll stop her before she starts, that will help mum" so I said "just shut up Jemima, because you are too young to understand" but it didn't work. Jemima shouted "what d'you mean about dad" and mum sort of scraped her fingers down over her face like she was trying to clean something off it, she said "perhaps we'd better just tell her, Lawrence, she has to know eventually."

That was new. I thought "all right then mum, if you say so." So mum did it. She told Jemima how dad tried to get into the cottage and how he turned all our neighbors against us, which was why we went to Rome. I was watching Jemima over Hermanns cage and I noticed her eyes were getting bigger and bigger so it was like they might go "pop" so I thought "uhoh" but Mum didn't stop. She said how Franseen was an enemy who told dad we were in rome, so he followed us, he came on rionair, and then she said how he did the strawberry cake and the nives in our beds and the poisson wisps in the water, which was why she couldn't have her baths. Now Jemima was making a funny little noise like a mouse, I think mum noticed too but she just went quicker, she said "so that's why we came to Scotland, we have to stop him once and for all you see, lamikin, its the only way." And then she said something else too, she made it sound nicer, like she was just making everything all neet and tidy, but she said it. She said what we were going to do now.

Everything was quiet for a moment. Mum was waiting, but I thought "uhoh" because it was like when the sea goes away before a big wave comes and bashes you. I thought "we should have just told her to shut up because she is too young to undestand, we should have said mum is just going off to the shop now to get her tea" but it was too late, because Jemima started, it was like the car was full up with her, first it was just a screem and then it turned into a word, it was "noo" she said "dads nice, he didn't do that."

Mum gave me a look, it was like she was saying "isn't she annoying" so I gave her one back saying "yes she is." I thought

"Jemima always has to reck everything" and it was funny, it was like our plan again now, it was me and mums, and I wasn't going to let Jemima spoil it. I thought "I wonder what we will do?" but it was easy actually. Mum didn't look worried, she said "you'll understand this later, lamikin, I know you will" then she pulled her head back out from between the chairs and suddenly I understood, I thought "oh of course, Jemima can't do anything anyway because she is all buckelled in." I thought "I will help mum" so I undid my seat belt, Jemima was screaming and trying to get out but of course she couldn't. So I got out and I closed my door to make her screeming a bit quieter. I was going to say "I'll get the petrol can mum" but I never did, actually, because that was when I notised a new thing.

You see there was a man standing there looking at mum. He had a jacket that was red and puffy like there were plastic bags in it, and he had a dog on a leesh which wasn't really small or big, it was inbetween, so I thought "wait a minite I know you, you are mister Andrews." He lived on dads street you see, his job was putting parking tickets on everybodies cars when they parked in the wrong place, dad said he was a bit of a drinker but he was all right really. Once when we were in a hurry and dad parked on a yellow line near the cheese shop he didn't give dad a parking ticket, he came into the cheese shop and told dad to move the car instead, which was nice. Now he looked really suprised, he looked at mum and he looked at the car with Jemima screaming and he said "Hannah, what are you doing here, whats going on?"

Mum smiled but it was funny, she looked like she wanted to shreek really, and she said "oh we were just passing, we've been up to the islands" which was a lie of course, we didn't go to any islands, we came from rome. Mister Andrews started saying "so are you not visiting . . ." but then he stopped and frowned, he looked through the window at Jemima because now she was shouting "don't mum don't mum don't" and I thought "mum looks worried, she looks scared, I bet she won't do anything now after all" I thought "that means this whole journey is just a big waste of time."

And that was when I had my brilliant idea. It was funny, because as soon as I thought of it I thought "oh yes, why didn't I think of it before?" because it was much better in every way you see, it meant everything would get done and they wouldn't be able to put mum in jail after all. Mr Andrews said "whats up with her?" his voice was all sort of mushy like it always was, dad said it was because he was a drinker, and I don't think he really noticed I was there, because I was on the other side of the car. So I crouched down a bit and I sneaked round to the back and when I tried the back door, it was open just like I hoped, because mum already opened it with the little handle on the floor by her feet. I thought "that's good"

It was a bit heavy but I pushed it up, it stayed open because it has little arms that hold it, and Mr Andrews was looking the other way, I could see his back, because he was talking to mum, that was good too. He said "she sounds bad, d'you think she should see a doctor?" and I understood that, mum said Jemima was screaming because she hurt herself. I reached in past all Jemimas silly dolls and pens that didn't work, and I got the plastic bag and the petrol can, it was really heavy but I got it, I thought

"I am strong" then I pulled them down and I sort of ran. I could hear them behind me, Mr Andrews said "Lawrence, hey where are you off to" and mum shouted "oh god Lawrence, no" and I looked back just for a moment, I could see her face, it was the one she got when she didn't know which way to go because me and Jemima ran off in different directions. She shouted "Lawrence" but I didn't take any notice, I thought "this will really help you mum, you just wait, you will be so pleased, you will say I'm so proud of you Lawrence."

I went straight across the road, I thought "this petrol can is heavy but Mr Andrews is old so he will be really slow, I will win" and then I had a good idea. I changed direction and went down a little lane that goes behind all the houses, I went down it once before, you see, dad said it is where the garbagemen come to take everyboddies rubbish. I thought "I bet Mr andrews didn't even see where I went" and I was right, because when I got to the other end I couldn't see him anywhere, he was gone. When I went out of the lane I looked all around, I was carefull and there wasn't anybody, I was safe. And suddenly I was there, I was right in front of dads house, so I thought "hurrah hurrah, you are clever Lawrence."

I looked in the bags, there was a packet of cloths which were white, there were matches and a big plastic funnel. I thought "what do I do?" because mum never really said you see, because she was supposed to do it, not me. I thought "uhoh, I am standing here, I'm not doing anything, seconds are going and soon mister Andrews will come or dad will come out, this is dreadful, this is a disaster." Then I thought "I suppose I have to put the funnel through the letter box" and I made my hands do it, but it was hard, actually, because the letter box wouldn't stay open, it hurt my finger. I thought "I will jam in the funnel, that will work" but the funnel just stuck out sideways so I thought "that's silly" and when I tried to pour some petrol down it, it didn't go in at all, it just sperted all over my shoes, I thought "oh mum, I don't understand, what was your plan?"

But I didn't give up, I tried again. This time I held the funnel a bit higher with one hand and with the other hand I did the petrol, I thought "I will do it really slowly and carefully" and though it was hard because it was so heavy, some went in, so I thought "oh yes, hurrah" and then I kept pouring it really slowly, I tipped it more and more, it took ages, until there wasn't any left, it all went in. That was wonderfull. So I put the petrol can down, I put the funnel back in the bag, and I got out one of the cloths. I thought "what do I do with this, I suppose I light it with the matches and then I drop it in."

So I tried, but that was hard too. It was because my fingers were funny and shaky, I thought "stop it fingers." The first match the end fell off, the second one lit but then it just went out again, and the third one lit but when I tried to light the cloth it went out, it made a tiny little smoke. Suddenly I got really annoyed, I thought "don't be silly now Lawrence, don't mess this up, you haven't got any time" so I did it really carefully. I lit the next match and I held it really still, I hardly moved it at all, I just put the cloth near and it worked, it started burning. So I thought "hurrah" I thought "that's all done" and I didn't wait at all, I didn't let myself, I just opened the letter box really wide and pushed it in.

And d'you know what happened? Nothing happened at all. I waited. I thought "now there will be a big noise" but there wasn't anything. So I opened the letter box again to see and then I understood, because you see dad had a kind of baskit made out of wires, it was there to catch all the letters and newspapers and stop them from falling on the floor and getting dirty. I thought "oh yes of course, why didn't I think of that, I often noticed it when I came and stayed for my weekends" because the cloth was just sitting in the baskit, you see, it was still burning a bit but it was stuck. I thought "oh no this is bad" I thought "why didn't you think of that mum?" I thought "perhaps it will help if I do another cloth" I couldn't think of anything else actually, so I got out another one and I was just going to try and light a match but then all sorts of things happened.

First there was Mister Andrews, who was running down the street towards me, I thought "how did you get all the way up there, you went the wrong way" he was on the pavement and he was shouting "Lawrence Lawrence." And then there was a car noise which was really loud like it was in a race so I thought "I bet that's mum" and it was. She braked very fast so she stopped just by dads gate and then she shouted through her window "get in Lawrence."

I felt so sad, I thought "sorry mum" because it was a real shame, we came all this way and it didn't work, I wasn't a hero after all, that was dreadfull. Mister Andrews was getting closer, even though he was old he was quite fast, actually, so I picked up the petrol can which wasn't heavy any more, I picked up the plastic bag and then I just ran to the car, mum was sort of leaning back so she could keep my door open. I got in really fast but Mister Andrews was right behind me, he shouted "hey stop" his dog was barking too, and then he grabbed mums door and pulled it open. I thought "what will I do?" I thought "you should have locked your door mum" but it was all right actually, because then mum pushed the door so he went back a bit and then she used it like it was a big stick, she hit him three times, it went "chump chump chump" and mister Andrews fell over, he hit his head a bit on another car so I thought "well done mum" I thought "poor mister Andrews."

But then something amazing happened. Because just as mum was shutting her door there was a funny noise, it went sort of "whuuump" and I knew what it was, I thought "oh yes this is wonderfull." Because, you see, the petrol lit after all, I don't know why, perhaps a bit of cloth dropped on it. When I looked back I could see a big flaime behind the little window in the door, it had colored glass and the flames made it look all flikery and pretty, so I thought "hurrah hurrah I did it."

But that was when everything went wrong. Maybe it was because mum was so tired after driving all the way from Rome, or it was because Jemima was screaming so loud. First mum made the car go forwards much too fast, and she didn't steer it properly either, so it hit the car in front of us and there was a noise of something going "smash" I thought "what was that, a head light?" After that she went backwards too fast as well, it was lucky that mister Andrews and his dog got out of the way, so we hit the car behind us now.

Finally we went forwards again, we went really fast, but now poor mum was steering completley wrong, she was shouting "oh god oh god" and we went sort of sideways right across the road so I thought "uhoh there is a wall" and we hit it I think, but I don't really know because I didn't have my seat belt done up, you see, so it was like I flew a bit and then I hit the seat in front. I thought "oh this feels funny" because I couldn't breath or anything, and I could hear mum shouting "no, no, no." She was trying to make the car go again but it just made a funny noise, it was like something was scrapping in the engine and the car didn't move at all.

I could hear a beeping, I think it was dads smoke alarm. Then we all just sat there. People came out of their houses and looked at us like we were really intresting. I could hear some sirens getting loud. I notised dad walking round his house, he came out from where he puts his garbage cans, his face was all dirty and black so I thought "he's all right then" and mum was screeming and screeming at the people "get him away, he's a murderer, he tried to poisson us, get him away, get him away." And suddenly I had a thought, I thought "oh dear, how on earth will we get back to Rome now?"

CHAPTER SEVEN

Nobody listened to what I said. In the ambulance I said "I have to go back to mum right now" but the lady policewoman didn't take any notice, I got so cross, she said "you've hurt your shoulder, Lawrence, you have to go to the hospital" and Mr Andrews didn't listen either, he was sitting there with his dog, he said "shes right laddie, you have to see the doctor." I said "but dad will get her, he tried to poisson us all" but they didn't take any notise, that was strange, that was dreadful, it was like they just didn't hear.

So we went to the hospital, we had to wait and wait, I couldn't bear it. After a while Mr Andrews went off to get his head done, which was a shame, I thought "he's nice, actually." I thought "what if somethings happened to mum, what if dads got her?" I thought "what if she gets lost so I can't find her?" The lady policewoman said "don't worry Lawrence, shes quite safe" but I thought "how d'you know, your not there, you're here."

Then I saw the doctor, he said my shoulder was all broken but I couldn't have a plaster because it broke in the wrong place, I could just have bandeges, which was annoying, because when Toby Miklaus broke his leg he got a plaster and everyone wrote their names on it.

Then it was time to go. I thought "oh good, hurrah, at last, now I will see mum." We drove for ages until we got to a big building, it was really quiet except I heard a man talking really loudly behind a door, and his voice sounded funny, he said "devels devels devels" so I thought "this is a stupid place, whats mum doing here?"

Then I went into my room and that was awful, that was a terrible thing, because mum wasn't there at all, you see, it was just Jemima. She jumped out of her bed like I was the best thing she ever saw, she grabbed my leg and she wouldn't let go. I said to the man who came with me "wheres mum?" but he just said "you rest now Lawrence, you'll see doctor Muckaye tomorrow morning and he'll explain everything." That made me so angry, I thought "he's not listening either." I said "I have to see her right now" but he just said "I'm really sorry but that's not possible" and then he did a horrible thing, he went out and locked the door.

The room was just white with a picture of horses in a field so it was like the Panda nuns room without any Jesuzes, and I thought "I'm not going to sleep, I will shout and shout" and I did shout for a bit, Jemima did too, we said "we want mum" but then I lay down on the bed, I didn't mean to, suddenly I just got tired. Jemima had her own bed but she didn't go in it, she came in mine instead, she lay there touching my back, and though it hurt my

shoulder a bit I let her. I thought "its nice shes here" I said "don't
worry Jems, everything's going to be all right."

The next morning a lady brought us breakfast, she said I had
to come and see doctor Muckaye, so I thought "about time too"
and I told Jemima "I'll be back soon, don't be scared." Doctor
Muckaye had tall black hair that came up off his head like a cliff,
it was like a big wave on the sea that got stuck, and I thought
"you are like your hair actually" because he was leening forward
at me with his arms folded like he was really intrested, his eyes
were looking right at me. I thought "its like you want to jump
forward off that chair" I thought "you are an eager beaver" I
thought "I think you are nice, I bet you will help us."

He said "how's your shoulder? You really hurt yourself there"
so I said "wheres mum, we have to see her right away." He did a
kind of frown like he was sad and he said "you have to understand
something, Lawrence, your mothers been very ill." Now I was
worried, I said "what d'you mean, in the car?" because there was
a sort of balloon that blew up when we crashed, I saw it, it was on
the steering wheel, I thought "maybe it bashed her head?" But
doctor Muckaye said "no I mean ill in a different way" so I said "it
doesn't matter if shes ill, I have to see her right now." And that
was when it happened. Doctor Muckaye looked sad again and he
said "I don't know how to say this to you, Lawrence, but I'm afraid
that's not a good idea right now. I can't let that happen."

I looked at him and suddenly I understood. I felt funny like I
went all cold in a fridge, I thought "I know who you are doctor
Muckaye, I know why you wont let me see mum, its because you
are a deadly enemy" I thought "how could I be so stupid, because

we are in Scotland now of course, dad has poissoned everyone against us." I was so cross, I wanted to shout out "you horrible traiter" but something stopped me, I don't know what it was, I think it was that cold fridge feeling. I looked at doctor Muckaye and I thought "you are pretending to be nice to cheat me" I thought "I will change your animal" which I don't usually do, I thought "you aren't an eager beaver any more, now you are a horrible black hairy spider in a big web" I thought "I don't know what nasty thing you want but I won't let you have it, I won't do anything you want."

What he wanted was for me to answer his questions and talk to him, so I thought "right, that's what I wont do." Not that it was easy, because when I didn't say anything he started looking all sad again, he said "Lawrence, I said hows your shoulder feel, why aren't you talking to me?" so I thought "all right I will say something" and I said "its fine." Then he gave me a look, he said "I understand if you feel angry towards me because I cant let you see your mother right now, but theres a reason for that" but I didn't ask about his reason, I didn't want to know, I just said "I'm fine" and when he said "all I want to do is help you. Is there anything you need? You must be feeling lonely" I just said it again, I said "I'm fine." I thought "this is good, because I can say this to everything" when he said "please talk to me Lawrence, you cant just keep saying 'I'm fine' " I looked at him and I gave him a real stare, but I smiled too, that was funny, I said "I'm fine."

After that I had to see Ann but I was ready for her now. She was thin with brown hair which was round like a hat, she had little glasses and she pretended to be nice too, she said "how're you doing, poor old Lawrence?" but then she said "so tell me about your journey to Rome" so I thought "I knew it, dad sent you as well, so you are a spider as well, you are a little brown one" I thought "you are like mr and mrs spider." Ann brown spiders questions were different from doctor Muckayes, they were all about driving on the motor way and not going to school, she said "weren't you sad to be missing all your lessons and your friends?" so I gave her a different aneswer, because "I'm fine" didn't work, I said "I don't remember." I didn't remember about leaving the cottage or going to Rome or anything, until Ann got a bit annoyed, she said "you don't remember very much, do you?"

Then it didn't work once, because she asked "did your mother hurt you, did she ever hit you, or your sister?" so I thought "that's horrible, how dare you, you horrible spider" so I said "no she didn't" and she gave me a look through her little glasses, and she said "so you do remember some things then, Lawrence?" she said "where did you stay when you drove to Rome, was it somewhere nice?" but I just gave her my look, I said "I don't remember." And it was funny, it was like mum was there with me, it was like she was sitting right beside me when I sat there saying "I'm fine" or "I don't remember" and she was saying "well done Lawrence love, I'm so proud of you."

Sometimes they talked to me and Jemima together but usually they did us just by ourselves. I told Jemima not to say anything, I told her they were enemies, but I think she forgot sometimes, because suddenly Ann spider knew lots of things. She said "and then you all slept all night in the car by the side of the road that time" and she said "and you just ate biscuits and drank fanta for two days, is that right, the car was full of rubbish like a trash can?" and though I said "I don't remember" I thought "oh dam dam" I thought "I don't know what you are doing Ann brown spider but I know its bad." Afterwards I told Jemima "what did you tell them?" and Jemima started crying, she said "I didn't tell them anything" which was a lie, I knew it, but I couldn't stay cross, I thought "your only a baby Jemima, you don't know" so I said "don't worry, its fine, your doing really well Jems, mum will be really pleased."

Once there was a surprise. Doctor Muckaye said "Lawrence I've got someone to see you" and it was dad. There he was standing looking at me with his funny smile like he didn't know what to say. Luckily I was all ready, I didn't wait at all, I just screemed really loudly "go away" and I wanted to throw something at him but there wasn't anything, there was just the sofa, that was too big. I said "I hate you dad, you tried to poisson us" and doctor Muckaye wispered something but I heard it, he said "I'm sorry, its too soon" so I shouted "no it isn't too soon, I don't ever want to see you again, not ever ever." I thought "you are pleased with me now mum, I bet." After that when I saw doctor Muckaye again he gave me a sad look and said "so your dad tried to poisson you, thats terrible, was this in Rome?" but I was ready again, I thought "I will change your answer now, black spider" so I said "I don't remember."

But it got harder. One day Docter Macaye was going on and on like usual, he was frowning and shaking his head, he said "why won't you talk to me Lawrence, all I want to do is help you, but I can't do that if you won't talk to me." My sholder was hurting again and I was really tired, I thought "please just shut up doc-ter Macaye" and then I made a plan. I thought "I know, I will just answer one of his stupid questions and that will make him stop talking, I won't say anything else, he will go away." So I did that, I said "your not trying to help me, you're an enimy." But it didn't work, because docter Muckaye didn't stop after all, he just gave me a look like I was sort of new now, and he said "why d'you say that Lawrence?" And it was funny, now that I told him one an-swer it was really hard to stop, I don't know why. I didn't mean to talk about mum, I didn't want to say anything, but somehow I did a bit, that was dreadfull, he tricked me.

Afterwards I felt so cross, I wanted to cry, I thought "mum wont be proud of me now." I went to our room and a funny thing happened, because though I didn't say anything it was like Jemima knew, because she stopped playing with the lego they gave us, it was big lego which is just for babies, I hadnt played with that for years, it just made walls, and she came and sat be-side me, she leaned against my arm. She said "hello Lawrence."

The next day something new happened. The door opened and in came Mister Simmons. I thought "oh this is good" because Mr Simmons was my favorite teacher at my old school, you see. I thought "he's not from Scotland so perhaps dad hasn't poisoned him against us, he isn't an enimy yet" I thought "I wonder if he's come to rescue us and take us to mum." He said "how are you then Lawrence, and you've hurt your shoulder, poor you" so I said "We have to find mum, we have to get away from here and go home to our cottage right away" but he gave me a funny look, he said "I'm afraid that's not possible just yet, Lawrence."

So I knew. I thought "that's just what doctor Muckaye says" and I felt so cross, I thought "and you were my best teacher." After that I didn't talk to him, I talked to Jemima instead, I said "this is mister Simmons, you remember him, he taught me writing" I said "and Henry Gibson says he smells of old farts, thats funny isnt it?" Jemima looked like she didn't know, but then she laughed a bit, and Mister simmons was blinking like he didn't know what to say, so I did some more, I thought "this is for you, traiter." I said "and Jemal Mustapha says hes the fattest teacher in the whole school, he says he's fatter than a zepplin, and Lidia Fitzroy says his jacket looks like he goes to sleep in it, she says its like his pyjamas, and his shoes are like dead moles." And though Mr Simmons stayed and talked more it was like all the air went out of him, so I thought "oh good you enimy, go away now."

One day after that something amazing happened. Docter Muckaye came to our room, he looked like he had a big secrit, he had something really new, and he said "someones come to see you." I thought "who is it now?" I thought "is it mrs Potter from next door or Franseen or Crissy Chick?" But it wasn't any of them. It was mum.

She looked really thin, she looked all tired, she was sort of leaning on the table. We just ran right at her, I got her waste and Jemima got her leg, and she hugged me so hard I could hardly breath. I thought "hurrah hurrah, everything will be fine now" I thought "hurrah hurrah, we won, we beat them all." Then mum sort of stood back a bit and she said "I've got something to tell you" and her eyes went blink blink blink so I said "what is it, are we going back to Rome now, is the car all fixed?" She said "no, its not that" and she looked funny like she had her headacke really badly, she said "I don't know how to say this. You see I got all mixed up, I'm afraid. I got all confused. Doctor Muckaye helped me to see that." This was bad, I thought "oh no, whats that spider done to you" and I said "what d'you mean mum?" and she said "I was all wrong about dad trying to hurt us. He wasn't even there. He was here in scotland all along."

I thought "this is new." But it was strange, because even though it was so new it was like a bit of me wasn't surprised actually, it was like a little bit of me knew all that already. I thought "what does it matter" I said "can we go home then? Where are we going, is it the cottage or back to Rome?" and Jemima shouted "Rome Rome." But mum gave us a funny look and her lips went sort of wobbley a bit like Jemimas do when shes going to cry, and she said "this is very hard for me to say, lesonfon, please don't make it harder than it already is" she said "I want you to forget everything I ever told you about your father, it was only because I was so confused. He's a good man."

Suddenly I had a nasty feeling, it was horrible, so I said "why do we have to do that mum?" She turned her head sideways like she was trying to hide, she said "because I want you to stay with him for a while." I felt like I couldn't breath, I think Jemima knew too because she was crying, so I said "but we don't want to, we want to stay with you." But mum wouldn't stop, she closed her eyes like she didn't want to hear us, she talked really fast like a shout, she said "I'm not going to discuss this. I've decided. Its better if you don't see me for a while, even a long while. Because I'm just not safe for you, you see. I don't trust myself. I might get confused again." It was just the horrible thing I guessed, and now Jemima and me were both shouting "no mum no" but she just wouldn't stop, she said "Your going to live with your father now. You have to do this. Its what I want."

SIENTISTS HAVE KNOWN FOR AGES that something terreble will happen to the sun. This is sad but there is nothing scientists can do, they can't stop it with any invention, even something really clever from the future, because the sun is too big you see, it will just happen anyway.

First it will run out of its fuel, that is like its petrol, it is hydrogen which is a gas. Then it will turn red and get bigger and bigger like a balloon, until it gets so huge that it will swallow any planets that are near, like mercury, they will just vanish. Earth won't get swallowed but it will get all burnt up, everything will go on fire, which is sad, there won't be anything left. If you could be there without getting burnt, if you built a special house with a special window, then you will be really suprised, because when you look up the sun will be so huge, it will go a third of the way across the whole sky. But then it will get smaller and smaller again until one day it will just go out. After that everything will be dark, so it will be like there's night all the time, it will be really cold.

But then scientists discovered a really good thing which is called gravitational lensing. Its when there is a galaxy quite far away in space, and it doesn't seem special at all actually, when scientists look at it through their telescopes they just think "so what?" But then one day there is a big surprise, because the galaxy moves a bit and the scientists all say "good hevens look at that." Because, you see, there were lots of other galaxies hidden behind it all the time that nobody saw. The other galaxies are right at the other end of the universe so you could never even see them usually, they are too far away, but when the near galaxy moves out of the way it does a funny thing. It sort of bends the light from the far away ones so they look big, its like it is a huge teliscope, so suddenly you can see them really well.

Perhaps the scientists will see another planet with their gravitational lensing, it will be lovely and green, it will be beautiful. Then everybody will be all right after all. They will build a huge space craft and escape there before the sun goes out.

So we went to live with dad in his new house, it was a bit bigger than his old one. Dad said we could each have our own bedroom but I said "no lets share a room, Jemima" and she said "all right Lawrence" because we did everything together now.

When we first went to dads house he was always trying to make us do things, he said "how would you like to go to the zoo today?" or "d'you fancy a ride out to the sea?" Sometimes I let us go but then I always changed my mind, when we got to the zoo I said "actually I don't want to go after all, I want to go home, don't you Jemima?" and she said "yes I want to go home too" because we did everything together. Dad never liked that, he said "but it'll be great, you can see all the animals, we can have lunch at the cafeteria" and he had his sad surprised look, so I thought "sometimes you are like a big dog who wants everyone to like you" and I just waited, I didn't say anything at all, until he gave in and said "all right, if that's what you want."

I had a new school now, they didn't like me at all. First it was because I sat at my desk and tore up pieces of paper so it made a noise and I went on doing it even when Mrs Gerald said I was disturbing the class. Then it was because I threw Kevin Mclusky's books into the loo. And after that it was because I hit Danny Monros head against the wall so it bled like a tiny little fountain, which was because I didn't like his ginger eye brows, they were so stupid and tufty. After that I had to see Mrs Moor the head-mistress, dad came too and he said I must be really good now or I would get expeled and I thought "oh yes, that will be funny" but I wasn't in the end, dad said "its been a very difficult time" and Mrs Moor said "this is your very last chance."

A few days after that when I got home dad was grinning like something was really good now, he said "I've got a surprise for you today Larry" and it was Hermann in his cage, dad said "I collected him from quorontine just this afternoon." I went over and looked and Hermann peered out through the bars so I thought "you remember me, Hermann, that's good." Jemima was shouting "Hermann Hermann" and dad was watching, he was waiting, so I thought "you want me to do something happy now, don't you dad" I thought "what will I say?" and then I thought "oh yes, that will be funny" so I said it, I said "Hermann this is dads house where we all live now" I said "I don't like it at all, I really hate it, actually, but there isn't anywhere else so we're stuck here." I wasn't looking at dad but I could sort of see him, actually, it was from the corner of my eyes, and it was like his smile fell right out of his face, that was funny. I thought "will I say something else?" and then I thought "no I won't."

Then one day we went to see my cousins in Glasgow. That was nice, their mum Susie made a lovely lunch, she said "eat up now Larry, we don't want you fading away to nothing" and afterwards we went upstairs to play. Charlie and Alice started doing a big puzzle with Jemima, it was of lots of things under the sea, and then Robbie said "shall we have a game of checkers then, Larry" and I said "okay." He took a white and a red draft and he hid them in his hands, he said "you choose" and I chose his right hand, it was white. Robbie started putting out his red checkers, he said "come on Larry" and I thought "I wanted to be red" I thought "I bet you cheated on that choosing Robbie." Then I thought "you have to teach these cheats a lesson" and I had a really funny idea, I picked up Robbies blue scalectric car which he always has to have because its his scalectric, I think its faster than the others, and I thought "I will make you into an airoplane." So I threw it right across the room and when it hit the floor some of the wheels came off, I thought "they are so stupid those scalectric cars, they just break."

Robbie was staring at me, they all were, he said "why the hell did you do that?" so I said "scalectrics so boring" and I had another really funny idea, I just kicked the track really hard so it jumped into the air, and then when Robbie ran at me I sort of got out of the way and pushed him a bit so he went right into the little table with his big leggo castle on it, that was funny too, because it fell off and broke into tiny bits.

After that dad didn't look like a dog who wanted everyone to like him, he had slit eyes and he said "this just cant go on." So we left Jemima with Nanna Edith and we went to see doctor Muckaye.

He said "so how are you, Lawrence?" and I thought "this will be easy" I said "I'm fine." After that he said "I hear you've been upsetting some people" so I said "I don't remember." We went on for a bit, I thought "this is fun" until then he gave me a look like he was really sad for me and he said "you must miss your mother very much." He said that before, actually, it wasn't new at all, so I wasn't surprised, I thought "what will I say, oh yes I'll say 'I'm fine' again" but then something funny happened. You see, suddenly I couldn't say anything at all because I was crying, I don't know how it got in, I tried to say "I'm fine" but it just didn't work, the words got all stuck.

That was strange, that was stupid. I thought "you tricked me you spider" and I said it, I said "I really hate you doctor Muckay." But he didn't get upset or angry like I wanted, he just gave me a long look and he said "I'm sorry to hear that, Lawrence" he said "why d'you feel like that?" and then something really really strange happened. Because I said something but I don't know where it came from, it was like somebody elses words just got in my mouth, they sneeked in. I said "I hate you mum." But Docter Muckay didn't look surprised even though I called him mum, that was funny, he just said in his usual voice "whys that Lawrence" and I felt so tired, it was like all my breathe was going out now, I said "because you left us. Because you are a traiter. Because you told me all those lies."

Later I went home in the car with dad, and we didn't say anything, I just looked at all the clouds, I thought "that one looks like a dog." He parked outside the house and I didn't move, I didn't undo my seat belt, and when he said "shall we go in then

221

Larry" I didn't say anything, I thought "I will just stay like this quite still." So we sat there for ages, that was funny, people walked past and sometimes they notised us and looked in, but we didn't say a word. Then eventually dad opened his door a bit, he said "I suppose I'd better start making our tea" and I thought "I'd better say something" so I made myself do it, I just did it, I said "I'm sorry I burned down your house dad" and he stopped, he gave me a little hit on my back but it didn't hurt, it was friendly, and he said "hey that's all right, Larry. I'm sorry about a lot of things too. I'm sorry I was away so much on all those stupid work trips." Then he said something intresting. He said "try not to be angry with her, Larry" he said "I know she and me didn't get on, it all went wrong, but I don't want you to hate her like this. It's not good for you." He said "she's not so bad, she just can't see things how they really are." That was new, that was different. I said, "all right, dad." I think about that sometimes.

A few days after that we went to the zoo, I let us go in this time, and it was nice actually. I thought "I wonder why I didn't let us come here before?"

After that everything became more like usual. In the morning dad knocks on our door and says "hey you lazy kiddies, time to get up" he makes our breakfast, toast and jam, and then he drives us to school in his yellow car, it has a stereo which mums didn't because it was broken, so we can listen to songs. Sometimes Nanna Edith collects us from school or we go to Sarah and Bill and Jimmy and Louisa till dad comes to get us. Sometimes we go to the sea for a few days, and its nice there, if its not raining you can see Mull and Sky. We often go and stay with my cousins in Glasgow, Robbie says he doesn't mind about the scalectric any more, the track was all right and he got a new blue car. Sometimes I think "actually they're nice all of these people" I think "I like having them." Its strange, sometimes its like I feel sort of sad because they're so nice to me. And sometimes I suddenly just feel really calm and still, I think "now I will be all right, yes, I will be all right now."

Hardly anyone ever talks about mum, Dad or my cousins, or my freinds at school. But I still think about her. I still sometimes think "are you going to come round that corner now mum? Are you going to get off that bus?" but she never is. Sometimes I'm really cross, its like I hate her, so I think "go away mum, I don't like you, I don't want you to get off that bus anyway." Sometimes I'm really sad, I think "I wish I could tell you about the funny thing Kevin Clark said at school." But mostly I just notice her. Because its like she suddenly starts talking to me, it can happen at any time. I am walking across the playground and she says "don't step in that puddle, Lawrence love, you'll get your shoes all wet" or I am in the supermarket with dad and Jemima and she says "put those crisps down, I've told you before, its not really bacon, its just chemicals" or I'm watching robot wars on television with Jemima and she says "that's enough telly, you know you two are turning into a real pair of couch potatoes."

I think Jemima hears her too, or she wouldn't play our secrit game. We don't do it often, just sometimes when we are at home and nobody is watching, when dad is downstairs on his computer or talking on the phone. Its like we both know even though we don't say anything, we just give each other a look, and Jemima has a funny smile like she is really pleased but she is worried too, because sometimes she doesn't like it, you see, sometimes she cries.

We go upstairs to our room, we sit on the floor and then I start. I say "d'you know Jemima, that window over there isn't real, it is just like a computer screen." Jemima always likes this bit, she giggels and says "what d'you mean, we're not in Scotland after all" and I say "thats right, Jemima, those houses and garden fences and television ariels aren't there, its really sky and rooves" I say "can't you hear the bells ringing?" Then Jemima laughs, she says "oh yes I can hear them, their really loud" so I say "now theres a tram going past, theres a police car with its funny siren, its like a donkey isn't it, and listen, theres someone talking in italian."

So we sit for a bit and then I do it more, I just like to, I say "d'you hear that little noise, Jemima, d'you know what that is?" Jemima doesn't really like this bit so she goes nervous, she says "no." But I go on anyway, I say "that's mums footsteps, shes right next door" I say "she'll come in here in a moment and she'll say 'come on lesonfon' because we're going out to get some pizza at the roasticheria." Then I say "what kind d'you want, Jemima?" If she answers its always the same, she says "I want tomato and cheese" but sometimes she doesn't say anything, she just sits there really still and her eyes go blink blink.

Then I sit back too. I close my eyes, we are just quiet for a bit, and d'you know its like we really are there. I feel sort of angry but I feel all calm too, that's funny. I think "it's a bit scary here but its nice" I think "its a real adventure" and I think "one day we'll all come back here again, mum and me and Jemima and dad, and we'll live here for ever and ever."

ACKNOWLEDGMENTS

I would like to give special thanks to Professor Raj Persaud, who kindly gave up so much of his busy schedule to read and reread the manuscript of this novel. I am wholly indebted to his shrewd and expert advice.

I would also like to thank Andrew Kidd, Nan Talese, Deborah Rogers, my wife, Shannon, and our children, Alexander and Tatiana.

"*A wryly comic, beautifully told seafaring yarn.*"
—Newsweek

ENGLISH PASSENGERS

In 1857, on the run from prying British Customs men, Captain Illiam Quillian Kewley is forced to put his ship *Sincerity* up for charter. The only takers are two eccentric Englishmen headed for the island of Tasmania: the Reverend Geoffrey Wilson, who believes the Garden of Eden was located there, and Dr. Thomas Potter, who is developing a sinister thesis about the races of men. And these passengers are only slightly odder than the crew, a diverse and lively bunch better equipped to entertain one another than to steer *Sincerity* across the Indian Ocean. Meanwhile, in Tasmania, an Aborigine named Peevay recounts his people's struggles against the invading British, who prove as lethal in their good intentions as in their cruelty. As the English passengers approach Peevay's land, their bizarre notions ever more painfully at odds with reality, we know a mighty collision is looming.

Fiction/978-0-385-49744-2

SMALL CRIMES IN AN AGE OF ABUNDANCE

A well-intentioned English family unwittingly becomes complicit in state violence while traveling through China. A ploddingly respectable London lawyer chances upon a stash of cocaine and realizes it offers the wealth and status he's always hungered for. A salesman in Africa gets caught up in a riot, and a Palestinian suicide bomber has a moment of self-doubt. Kneale transports readers across continents in a nanosecond, reaching to the heart of far-away societies with rare perceptiveness. With wry humor and razor-sharp satire, these twelve thought-provoking stories illuminate the moral uncertainty of our time.

Fiction/978-1-4000-7957-5

ANCHOR BOOKS
Available at your local bookstore, or visit
www.randomhouse.com